Baffled at Bristol

by

Cynthia Moore

Road To Romance, Book 4

Baffled at Bristol

Cover Art by *Tina Lynn Stout*

The Wild Rose Press, Inc.
PO Box 708
Adams Basin, NY 14410-0708
Visit us at www.thewildrosepress.com

Publishing History
First Edition, 2024
Trade Paperback ISBN 978-1-5092-5469-9
Digital ISBN 978-1-5092-5470-5

Road To Romance, Book 4
Published in the United States of America

Dedication

To my sister-in-law Kamaryn. She loves reading and the United Kingdom as much as I do.

Chapter One

Mid-April 1820, Bristol

"My goodness, ladies! We have accomplished an inordinate number of tasks today. We deserve a lavish tea." Aunt Prudence handed several parcels to a waiting servant.

"I am eager to take off my bonnet and sit down for a while," Ellen responded, with a sigh.

"May we stop at the circulating library for one moment, Mother?" her cousin Abigail pleaded. Shy and reserved, Abigail had exhibited a short, plump form as a child, which had given way to a lithesome, slender physique once she turned eighteen. Now twenty, her black locks, inherited from her father, were gathered into a tight bun on the crown of her head. Short, curling strands hemmed the sides of her face and dangled across her forehead. She had wide, dark brown eyes framed by thin, ebony brows, an angular nose with an unfortunate inward curve at its tip, and a small mouth with a protruding lower lip.

Aunt Prudence reached up to tuck a wayward strand of her thick, blonde hair, mingled with a few strands of gray, underneath the brim of her wide-brimmed straw hat. A plume of ostrich feathers, attached to the front of the high crown, fluttered in the gentle breeze. "As long as you promise to put your books away periodically and make an effort to meet eligible gentlemen."

Abigail's smooth, translucent complexion turned rosy. "Yes, Mother. I promise."

"We must find a man with good prospects for you as well, Ellen," her aunt resolved. "Come along now."

Ellen frowned at the ground as she and Abigail strolled behind her. Aunt Prudence fancied herself a matchmaker, believing her unique aptitude and comprehension of personalities led to marriages of lifelong love and happiness. She insisted it was her support and encouragement that brought Ellen's parents together. Her Uncle George, Aunt Prudence's late husband, humored her good-intentioned pastime while he was alive, but shortly after her year of mourning for him was over, the harmless diversion had become an obsession. Her cousin often wrote to her lamenting her mother's obtrusive manner. Ellen recalled part of one especially poignant sentence…*for Mother will give her opinion on the couple's suitability to their faces!* Up until now, she and Abigail had avoided becoming targets for her well-meaning meddling. It appeared they would no longer be spared.

"Mrs. Pratt!" a short, hefty young lady with round, dimpled cheeks and thick red hair, tucked most ineffectively underneath a hat with a broad rim, called out. She stood on the other side of the street.

"May we speak with you a moment, Mrs. Pratt?" A tall, lean man turned to smile warmly down at the woman by his side before attentively escorting her across the road, his short, curly blond hair fluffed by the breeze.

"Of course. Good day to you both! I haven't seen you since your wedding day a few months ago." She turned to Ellen and Abigail. "You have met my daughter.

This is my niece, Miss Cather. She comes to visit us every spring. This is Mr. and Mrs. Hunter."

"It is lovely to make your acquaintance, Miss Cather. Wonderful to see you, Miss Pratt." Mrs. Hunter smiled, holding out her gloved hand to Ellen and then Abigail, before turning once more to face her aunt. "We wished to express our thankfulness and gratitude once again to you, Mrs. Pratt!"

"Yes, indeed! I never imagined I could know such jubilation." The man looked down with a fervent expression at his wife, placing his free hand on top of hers as it rested on his forearm.

"When I recall how convinced I was that we should never suit…" Mrs. Hunter giggled as she gazed adoringly up at her husband and batted her eyelashes.

He chuckled. "Observe how different we are! We believed we had nothing in common. But you, Mrs. Pratt, held firm and advised us to disregard outward appearances, to appreciate the person inside."

"It is lovely to hear you are both content and happy. I hope I don't offend and sound obnoxiously forward when I say I am not surprised." Aunt Prudence grinned and waved at them as they said their goodbyes. She turned back to Ellen and Abigail. "Well! I must say, I never tire of receiving news of the joyful unions I orchestrated."

"Mother! Look who I met strolling about the streets of town—my school chum from Eton, Mr. Henry Stanhope and his friend Mr. John Rudder!" Ellen's other cousin, brother to Abigail, Mr. Thomas Pratt, hailed them from a short distance away.

Ellen studied the three men as they walked across the road to join them. Her cousin Thomas was of medium height and slender, with thick hair in a similar hue as his sister's. He had a guileless, pleasing countenance. Mr. Stanhope was short and stout. He had a thatch of red hair covering the top of his head and a pale complexion with a dusting of freckles across the tip of his nose and on his cheekbones. Mr. Rudder was tall and muscular, the tight sleeves on his coat accentuated his robust forearms. He had thick, wavy brown hair brushed forward in the popular Caesar style and wide sideburns framing the sides of his face. All three gentlemen were dressed fashionably in tailcoats and pantaloons, with elegantly tied cravats at their necks. Thomas quickly performed the introductions. Mr. Stanhope acknowledged the others before bowing to Ellen.

"It is wonderful to come across you again, Miss Cather."

She curtsied to him. "I am happy to see you as well."

"The two of you are already acquainted?" Aunt Prudence asked, with raised brows.

"Yes, we are." Ellen's heart pounded painfully hard inside her chest as she noted her aunt's sly expression. "We were both guests at a county retreat almost two years ago at Horsham House, Sir Edward Collins's estate."

"I see. And what brings you to Bristol, Mr. Stanhope?" her aunt inquired, with a pointed look at Ellen.

"A group of fellow rowing enthusiasts are meeting here to participate in a regatta, ma'am. It is to be held a week from Saturday," he explained. He turned to face his companion. "Mr. Rudder, you do recall Miss Cather from our time at Horsham House?"

Mr. Rudder turned to her, his hazel eyes glowing

like wet moss after a spring rainstorm. "It is wonderful to see you again, so soon after the wedding. Of course, I remember the grand time we had in the country. What brings you here, Miss Cather?"

"I am gratified to meet you again as well," she replied, before taking a deep breath to calm her fluttering pulse. "I come to Bristol each spring for a visit. Mrs. Pratt is my aunt. And this is my other cousin, Miss Abigail Pratt."

He turned to face them, doffing his top hat, bowing in a gallant manner. "Quite happy to make your acquaintance, Mrs. Pratt and Miss Pratt."

"You both attended a wedding recently?" Aunt Prudence smiled and briefly closed her eyes as she clasped her gloved hands against her broad chest. "How lovely and romantic! May I be apprised of those for whom the ceremony was held?"

Ellen cleared her throat before answering, uncomfortable with her aunt's overly excessive reaction. "My dear friend Miss Camille Collins married Lord Frederick Surd. They were also guests at the Horsham House gathering."

"Lord Surd is a good friend of mine as well," Mr. Rudder clarified.

"The country house party sounds as if it must have been quite an exhilarating diversion." Her aunt studied them both for a several moments before continuing, "Are you also in the city to compete in the rowing event Mr. Stanhope was just describing to us, Mr. Rudder?"

"Yes, I am. Mr. Stanhope requested I join his crew."

She chuckled and rubbed her gloved hands together. "My daughter, niece, and I have finished an exhaustive day of shopping. We intend to return home to enjoy an abundant tea. You gentlemen must come along and join us."

"What…What about the circulating library, Mother?" Abigail questioned in an imploring tone.

"It will have to wait, my dear."

Mr. Rudder frowned. "I am sorry, but we are unable to join you for tea, Mrs. Pratt. Mr. Stanhope and I have a prior engagement with two gentlemen who are also on our rowing team."

"May I inquire where you are meeting them?" Aunt Prudence asked.

"At a tavern called The Lamb and Anchor," Mr. Stanhope informed her.

"Nothing could be simpler! Come along with us," her aunt answered, with a boisterous titter. "We reside a few blocks from there, off Queen's Square."

"I will gladly escort Miss Pratt to the library and squire her home after her errand is completed," Mr. Rudder offered.

Abigail's brown eyes widened. "Thank you, sir, for your kind offer, but it would be unseemly to accompany you. I-I do not have my maid with me."

"Nonsense!" Aunt Prudence objected loudly. "We will take Prince Street and all walk to the library together, a minor divergence from our journey home. You may conduct my daughter inside while the rest of us dally out in front, Mr. Rudder. I have no doubt the task done in this manner would be above reproach."

"I say! May I join you both at the tavern?" Thomas inquired. "I haven't rowed for several years, since I attended Eton, but I would like to hear your plans for participating in the regatta."

Mr. Stanhope raised his brows and looked at Mr.

Rudder before replying, "Certainly you may come with us."

They soon arrived at the library. Mr. Rudder offered his arm to Abigail, and the two of them strode up the front steps, disappearing inside. While waiting outside, Ellen kept up a desultory conversation with her aunt regarding the prospects for a warm spring while Thomas and Mr. Stanhope discussed the merits of the *catch* and *release* rowing strokes. Abigail and Mr. Rudder emerged from the building a few minutes later, smiling warmly at each other. He carried two slim volumes tied with string in one hand. Her fingers clutched his free arm as he guided her down the front stairs.

"It appears your task was completed in an agreeable manner," Aunt Prudence observed, with an arch grin.

"We had no difficulty in finding the books I wanted, Mother. Apparently, poetry has become less favored reading material upon publication of the latest Gothic romance."

"I was impressed with Miss Pratt's choices. Coleridge and Wordsworth are favorites of mine as well," Mr. Rudder remarked, as he followed the others down the street. "Are any of you aware Wordsworth lived near Bristol with his sister?"

"Yes, I am. He and his sister Dorothy first stayed with Mr. Cottle on Wine Street in 1798. I believe they moved shortly afterward and resided west of here in a place called Alfoxton Park," Thomas answered. "I recall they spent only one year there. Coleridge also came to Bristol a few years earlier, in 1794."

"Do you enjoy reading Gothic romances, Miss Cather?" Mr. Stanhope asked, as he strolled along beside her.

She smiled at him before replying. "I admit I have read *The Mysteries of Udolpho*. However, it failed to cause my palms to sweat or my heart to race in fear. I understand a terrifying experience is one of the main attractions when perusing Gothic works. I prefer non-fiction books on the history of famous cities and their architecture. I read an excellent book on Bath last year."

Mr. Stanhope frowned. "Surely construction and building structure are arduous, knotty topics for a lovely, young woman such as yourself. I imagine books covering the prevailing modes and wardrobes from Paris would be more appropriate. However, if you wish to indulge in a satisfying tale attested to frighten the reader, may I recommend the story of Frankenstein? I read it last winter and it made a lasting, dark impression on me."

"Indeed? I have heard several other people speak favorably of the story. I believe I will read *Frankenstein*. Thank you very much for your suggestion."

He bowed to her, rising with an engaging grin on his face. "You are quite welcome. Promise me you will put the book down if it should give you nightmares."

Ellen chuckled. "It would take much more than a fanciful Gothic story to torment me in such a way."

"I am quite relieved to know that."

"Pardon me, I overheard you both discussing the novel *Frankenstein*," Abigail commented as she walked up to Ellen's side. "I understand there is a debate over the identity of the author. Some believe the daughter of William Goodwin wrote the tale."

Mr. Stanhope raised his brows. "I have no knowledge of such a discussion, but it has been mentioned the story was crafted after a challenge was made between several aspiring authors to write a unique tale of horror."

"Quite fascinating!" Abigail turned to her. "You must tell me what you think of the book after you have finished it, Ellen."

"We have arrived," Aunt Prudence announced, as they came to a stop in front of their townhouse. "Thank you, gentlemen, for your escort. May I invite you both to tea tomorrow?"

Mr. Stanhope stared at the ground before replying, "The regatta is next Saturday. Until then, the mornings, except for Sunday, will be taken up with practice. We would need to change our clothing…"

"No matter. Perhaps another day, once you have determined your schedule. May we come watch the drills?"

"Yes, you may. We will be on the course tomorrow a little after ten o'clock, on the other side of Spike Island at the New Cut portion of River Avon," Mr. Rudder informed them, with a smile.

Aunt Prudence bobbed her head to both men. "It has been a pleasure. We look forward to attending the practice. Thomas will direct you to the tavern at the end of this lane. Ladies, take your leave of the gentlemen."

Ellen stepped forward, offering her gloved hand to Mr. Stanhope. "Good evening. It was lovely meeting you again."

He clutched her hand and bowed over it, before standing straight and smiling down at her. "I am ecstatic at the chance to renew our acquaintance, Miss Cather."

"Thank you." She turned to face Mr. Rudder and stifled a groan when her cheeks suddenly felt as if they were on fire. "I-I am quite happy to see you once more."

He reached for her hand, grinning. "Indeed. A

providential occasion to further our association. I too have an interest in architecture. We must find a time to discuss the book on Bath."

"Abigail?" Aunt Prudence tapped one foot up and down against the ground and jutted out her chin.

Abigail slowly moved forward from her position behind Ellen, curtsying to Mr. Stanhope. "I am happy to have made your acquaintance."

He bowed to her. "And I as well."

She then faced Mr. Rudder. "I am pleased to have met you. Thank you for accompanying me to the library."

He bowed and held out the books. "You are quite welcome, Miss Pratt. I look forward to hearing your views on Wordsworth's poetry. A favorite of mine refers to daffodils."

"Oh! How lovely!" Abigail giggled. "I am quite partial to those flowers."

Aunt Prudence beamed a radiant smile at her daughter and turned toward the doorway. "Good evening, gentlemen. We will see you both tomorrow. Don't be too late, Thomas."

Ellen glanced at Mr. Rudder to discover him staring at her. His hazel eyes widened as their gazes met. Mortified, she twisted around, quickly striding up the steps, following her aunt and cousin inside.

The butler, Griggs, was waiting in the entryway. He took their wraps and hats before informing them tea had been placed in the drawing room.

"Wonderful!" Her aunt chuckled as she turned and made her way down the corridor. "Goodness, it has been an exhilarating day! I am quite parched."

Ellen and her cousin entered the room behind her.

Aunt Prudence lowered her portly frame onto the sofa with a sigh before reaching for the teapot. She poured the hot beverage into the cups. "My dears! Such a fortunate circumstance to have a regatta taking place in the city! And both of you made an instant conquest of the gentlemen!"

Ellen lowered her brows in consternation as she took a seat in a chair across from her. "Not at all, Aunt! You are imagining the extent of the impression we made on them."

Aunt Prudence smiled as she held out a cup to her. "You are quite modest, my dear! It was a simple matter to note Mr. Stanhope's interest in you. And Mr. Rudder! He was most gracious to Abigail. You met them both previously, Ellen. Who are their families? Do they come from prosperous stock?"

"Mother!" Abigail's cheeks flushed red as she lowered herself onto the sofa.

"I am certain Thomas will vouch for them. However, it is quite proper for me, a widowed lady and a close relative, in the absence of her parents, to inquire as to their circumstances before allowing either gentleman to court Ellen." She placed a cup on the table in front of Abigail.

"You exaggerate the situation, Aunt. I have simply renewed a previous acquaintance and Abigail has just been introduced." Ellen took a sip of tea.

"I have no intention of letting such an exceptional opportunity pass by." Aunt Prudence reached for an apple tart, bit off a large chunk, and chewed on the pastry for several seconds. "Since your formal introductions to society over two years ago, I have stood back and allowed both of you freedom to make your own choice.

No prospective suitors have come forward. It is past time I brought my expertise to the table. You know nothing more of these gentlemen, Ellen?"

She sighed, realizing her aunt was not to be dissuaded. "I believe Mr. Stanhope is the son of Viscount Preen and Mr. Rudder is the son of Viscount Tilbrook. I have no other knowledge of their families or financial situations."

"Both sons of viscounts! How thrilling! Mr. Stanhope strikes me as a loyal, steadfast person. Mr. Rudder is obviously quite handsome with excellent refinement, not at all affecting. I will continue to study each of their mannerisms and affectations to determine which gentleman is your true counterpart. Examine your wardrobes this evening, ladies. Decide which walking gown is most flattering to your complexions. Request Fanny to assist you. Sleep well tonight. It is imperative to appear as radiant as possible and present yourselves with delightful, beguiling singularity without airs. If this is accomplished, you will certainly charm both men after the race practice tomorrow."

Chapter Two

As he scraped the razor blade across the cluster of whiskers under his chin, John stared at himself in the room's tiny mirror. He noted the dark, shaded indentions under his eyes. It had been a chore to get to sleep last night. With a final swipe at a spot underneath his nose, he rinsed the razor, dropped it onto the counter, and reached into the bowl of water. He splashed his cheeks and chin with the cool liquid before wiping his face dry with a towel. He hung the towel on the rack next to the washstand and picked up his boar-bristle toothbrush, sprinkling a bit of toothpowder on it before popping the brush into his mouth and quickly polishing his teeth. After completing that task, he put the toothbrush onto the counter next to his razor and walked across the room to confront the pile of extensively used clothing he had removed from his bag and tossed on the foot of the bed the night before.

With a sigh, he reached for a linen shirt with frayed cuffs, pulling it over his head and tucking the ends into the waistline of his shabby, faded breeches. The breeches had served him well during a few cricket matches in Hampshire last summer. He volunteered to replace a player who had to leave the event when he learned his father was extremely ill. After securing the buttons on the front flap of the breeches, he studied the pile of colored, folded neckcloths that supplemented standard sailor's attire. He purchased them from an enterprising shopkeeper near the docks in London. John chose a sea-green one, tying it in a haphazard fashion around his neck, and then opened the top drawer of the bureau, picking out a pair of white stockings. Many seasoned rowers chose to go without them, considering it less troublesome if water splashed into the boat and got their shoes wet. John preferred to have his feet and ankles protected. He walked across the room to sit on one of the two high-backed Windsor chairs gracing the sparsely furnished room. Bending over, he pulled a stocking over each foot, then up his ankle and calf. His scuffed, black leather pointed-toed shoes with rectangular buckles were on the floor nearby. Standing up, stepping into the shoes, he paused for a moment to stare out the window.

They had been lucky to find two rooms vacant at the lodging house on the corner of Baldwin Street and Colston Avenue, considering the number of spectators expected to come to the city to watch the boat races later in the week. He could just make out bits of spray as the water from the Floating Harbor splashed upon the rocks along Broad Quay. As he studied the scene outside, his thoughts strayed once again to the conundrum that had kept him awake last night, the surprising emergence of Miss Cather in Bristol.

He thought about the last time he had seen her, in March, at the wedding in London. She took his breath away when he strode inside the chapel just before the ceremony was set to begin. She stood at the back of the church having a low-voiced discussion with Lady Millington. Miss Cather's thick blonde hair was drawn up high on the crown of her head. A long braid, threaded with pink myrtle blossoms, encircled the closely gathered strands. Loose ringlets framed her delicate, angelic features, complimented by pale blue eyes, a thin, diminutive nose, and perfect bow-shaped lips. Her gown, the color of a ripe summer peach, was a splendid adornment for her willowy gracefulness. The sleeves were short and full, set with bands of matching satin and edged at the bottom with delicate lace. He recalled noticing the base of her skirt when someone opened the door, allowing a gust of wind inside the chapel. The one flounce, decorated with narrow bands of satin, had rippled in the breeze, accentuating a row of four-sided diamond configurations along the border.

After the ceremony finished, the guests gathered at Sir Edward's townhouse to celebrate. Abundant glasses of champagne were offered by a group of industrious footmen along with lemon tarts and precisely cut pieces from an almond cake decorated on top with powdered sugar and currants. John attempted to speak with Miss Cather to discuss their mutual friends and her recent trip to Bath with Lady Surd, but every time he spotted her standing by herself, she was quickly joined by another acquaintance.

John hoped to meet Miss Cather at a ball or find her strolling through Hyde Park upon returning to London after the regatta. Now he had been handed a fortuitous opportunity. He intended to accept her aunt's invitation to tea and determine other ways to spend time in her company when he finished with the imperative daily practice. John put a hand to his forehead, massaging the throbbing pulse just underneath his hairline that threatened to turn into a headache. At present, he needed to concentrate on the upcoming race on Saturday and today's training.

He reached for his horsehair brush and ran it through his thick locks before turning to shove his arms into the sleeves of a tattered, dark-gray coat that he had discovered, tucked away for a chance purpose such as this, in the back of his dresser at home. On the way to the chamber door, John reached for the floppy, straw hat, used during his Harrow schooldays, that was balanced atop the bedpost. He caught his reflection in the mirror and grinned, thinking of his valet's reaction if he were to spot him in his current attire.

He walked out into the passage and made his way down the rickety stairs to the breakfast room. It was empty. The hands on the clock on the mantel, over the fireplace on the other side of the room, pointed at a few minutes after nine o'clock. Several covered dishes, two baskets of sliced bread, and a stack of mugs were atop a table nearby. Two rectangular tables, seating six each, dominated the center of the room.

"Good day, Mr. Rudder! Would you prefer coffee or tea?" The proprietor, Mrs. Dowding, came bustling into the chamber carrying two large vessels. "There are eggs, slices of ham, and bits of boiled potato in those dishes. Help yourself."

"Good morning. I will have coffee." He pulled out a chair at the end of one of the tables and sat down, placing his hat on the table.

Mrs. Dowding positioned the two pots next to the baskets of bread, reached for a mug, and poured coffee into it. She set the full cup on the table in front of him. "Here you are, sir."

"Thank you." He took a gulp of the hot beverage before hearing pounding footsteps coming down the stairs.

"Good morning! I will have coffee as well, Mrs. Dowding." Mr. Stanhope strode through the door, clutching in one hand a rumpled, round hat with a narrow brim. His short, stocky legs were covered with loose trousers, embellished with side pockets. Unlike John's breeches, which fit snugly over his knees, Mr. Stanhope's trousers descended his legs to lie slack, just above his ankles. He sported a bright yellow neckcloth dangling over what was once a vivid red-and-yellow horizontally striped, single-breasted waistcoat, now faded from frequent use or perhaps many washings. His double-breasted coat had brass buttons and closed mariner's cuffs. A watch fob hung at his waist. No stockings appeared over the tops of his grazed, black leather shoes with rounded toes and oval-shaped buckles. He dropped his hat on the table next to John's and turned to study him. "I see you managed to rig yourself out in proper sailor's attire. Well done!"

"Good day! I discovered several garments that would serve the purpose in my bureau at home. I was obliged to purchase a few neckcloths." John got up from his chair to stroll with Mr. Stanhope to the food table while Mrs. Dowding poured coffee into another cup.

"Let me know if you gentlemen require anything else," the landlady called out from the doorway. "Ring the bell and I will come."

"Thank you, ma'am." Mr. Stanhope spooned a pile of potatoes onto his plate before lifting the cover off the dish of ham. "Quite a substantial spread, don't you agree?"

"Quite adequate," John concurred. He waited to speak again until they both filled their plates and sat down. "I'm glad you came downstairs early. I wished to obtain more information from you about our rowing mates."

"What did you wish to know?" Mr. Stanhope cut a piece of ham and popped it into his mouth.

"I am specifically concerned about Mr. Thorne. He was clearly bosky when he arrived at the tavern yesterday, and after several tankards of ale, he was thoroughly foxed by the time we left. In order to make a good showing in the race, everyone on our team should be fit and alert."

Mr. Stanhope flushed and swallowed before speaking. "I noticed that as well. Both Mr. Thorne and Mr. Campbell come highly recommended. You recall, they are members of the Westminster School Boat Club and have participated in several rowing events on the Thames."

"That boat club certainly has an excellent reputation. When you inquired about their familiarity with the rules and requirements of the race soon after they joined us last night, both appeared quite knowledgeable. Do you know how long they have been members?"

Mr. Stanhope furrowed his brows and spooned the remaining eggs and potatoes into his mouth. He chewed for several moments without speaking. "I recall something Mr. Campbell mentioned about a race they participated in last summer. Their boat took second place. No, I do not remember hearing how long it has been since they joined the club."

John put his fork onto his empty plate and took a swig of coffee before reaching into his coat pocket for his tin holding comfits. He flipped open the lid and popped a confection into his mouth.

"What is that?" Mr. Stanhope inquired, staring at the tin.

"They are called comfits, bits of spices compressed together. My uncle works for the East India Company. He discovered them on one of his travels to India. This is clove. They are also made with cinnamon, anise, peppermint, and ginger. I find they clean my palate and freshen my breath after I eat. Would you like to try one?"

Mr. Stanhope reached inside the tin, picked out one of the hard bits, and popped it into his mouth. "Quite an unusual flavor."

"They are refreshing. I have quickly formed a dependence on them." John replaced the container inside his pocket and came to his feet. "Perhaps Mr. Thorne was excited about the upcoming racing event and drank to celebrate yesterday. We must closely observe him today. I trust he won't do something embarrassing and throw a rub in the way of our efforts to make a good showing. If you are finished, we should make our way to the boathouse."

Mr. Stanhope stood up from the table and reached inside his coat pocket, pulling out a piece of vellum with writing on it. He studied the sheet for a moment before folding it and putting it back in his pocket. "I wished to remind myself of the location and the name of the person we check in with."

They quit the breakfast room and walked down the corridor to the front entry. John swung open the door.

"Good day! I thought I'd walk with you and watch the process of placing the boat in the water." Thomas Pratt hailed them from the street outside. He sported a hat with a wide brim turned up on both sides, a cream-colored neckcloth, single-breasted gray jacket, and loose-fitting, faded brown breeches without stockings. His feet were covered with scuffed, round-toed shoes.

"Good day, Mr. Pratt!" Mr. Stanhope called, as he walked up to him.

"Morning." John studied his attire. "You look prepared to jump into a boat and start rowing. Are you certain you aren't on one of the opposing teams?"

"No, no!" He chuckled. "I dug these breeches out of the bottom of an old chest. I haven't worn them since my last race at Eton, four years ago. Thankfully, they still fit. I thought I should look the part even if I'm not competing."

"Happy to have you come along." Mr. Stanhope gestured to the right. "This way. The boathouse is in the dry dock just off Prince Bridge near Bathurst Basin. We are to speak with a Mr. Burke. The others are to meet us there."

They strode down Colston Avenue to where it intersected with Marsh Street and crossed the Market Square to Prince Street and then on to the drawbridge.

It was a short distance from the end of the bridge to the dry dock, where John spotted a stooped man standing in front of a brick-sided boathouse. He had dim, black eyes that scrutinized them from a wrinkled, sun-weathered face. The man gripped a piece of torn parchment in his hand.

John walked up to him. "Mr. Burke?"

The man furrowed his bushy brows and studied him intently. "Yes. You be here for one of the boats? What's your name?"

"My name is Rudder." He turned to the others. "This gentleman is Mr. Stanhope."

Mr. Burke squinted down at the rumpled sheet of

parchment. "And you? Mr. Thorne or Mr. Campbell?"

"Neither, sir," Mr. Pratt answered. "I'm just a spectator."

Mr. Burke frowned. "Where are the other two men? I can't allow you to take the boat until all your crew is present."

"Sorry to be late, gentlemen!" Mr. Campbell came to an abrupt stop in front of their group, panting.

"This is Mr. Campbell." John frowned at his attire, obviously thrown on in an aimless manner. His neckcloth was lopsided, one end hanging down limply across his heaving chest. A battered hat covered his head, the brim bent and flopping across the back of his neck. "Where is Mr. Thorne?"

Mr. Campbell flushed as he tugged at the front fastenings on his double-breasted coat. "He will be along shortly. I had a devil of a time waking him up this morning."

Mr. Burke grunted and turned to step inside the boathouse. "You gents ain't attending a tea party. This here is a set practice time. You get one opportunity each morning before the day of the race to prepare. Your starting time is ten o'clock. All the crew need to be present. You will have to come back tomorrow."

John's stomach muscles clenched, and he tasted bile in the back of his throat. They dare not lose any of their few chances to prepare for the regatta. "Wait! Mr. Pratt is our alternate crew member. May we practice with him today?"

Mr. Burkes studied his list. "I don't see his name here."

"We…We weren't certain if we were allowed to have substitute crew members. We brought him along

21

should one of us become injured." John quickly fabricated the reason and then held his breath.

"Hmmm." Mr. Burkes glared at them from underneath his brushy brows. "I will put him down as a temporary crew member for today only. Make certain Mr. Thorne is here tomorrow at ten o'clock sharp. Your boat is there on the rack to the left. Her name is Scamper. Ignore the crafts on the right wall. They are the wherries we keep here for pleasure boating. Choose your own oars. They are stacked along the back wall. Leave them with the boat when you return it shortly after eleven o'clock."

"Thank you for making the exception, sir. Come along, gentlemen." John led the way to the boat lying on the rack Mr. Burke had indicated. "Mr. Stanhope, you and Mr. Pratt take the far side. Mr. Campbell and I will lift the other. Let's place it in front of the boathouse while we chose our oars."

Once the selection of oars was made and tossed inside the boat, they carried Scamper down a slight incline to the dock at the entrance of Bathurst Basin.

"I apologize for failing to procure your consent to be part of our crew today, Mr. Pratt," John told him. "I trust you are comfortable joining us?"

"A pleasure. I am happy to be of assistance." Mr. Pratt chuckled. "I certainly understand the need to practice. Allow me a few preliminary strokes to accustom myself to the rhythm."

"Are you and I maintaining the same positions we eventually decided upon last night?" Mr. Stanhope asked as they lowered the boat onto the dock. "Recall Mr. Thorne was bent on occupying the rear stroke position."

"We now have clear evidence of the calamity that

would have occurred if we had agreed to his demands. Nothing has changed as far as our initial strategy is concerned. You are the more experienced rower and have ample upper body strength. You maintain the bow position. I am comfortable with setting the stroke rate and rhythm and will occupy the stroke seat." John turned to the others. "Mr. Pratt, since it has been several years since you rowed, I would suggest you take the seat directly behind Mr. Stanhope. Mr. Campbell will cover the spot in front of me."

They placed the light, wooden craft into the water. John held the stern steady against the dock while the others took their seats in the boat. Once they were settled, he waited for Mr. Stanhope to grasp the edge of the dock before he jumped in and settled in his position at the stern. He quickly inserted his oars inside the swivel oarlocks on either side of the boat and then nodded to a man standing nearby waiting to cast them off. "Ready!"

The boat quickly floated out into the gushing current of water heading toward the New Cut portion of the River Avon.

"Start your catch, gentlemen!" John yelled over the roar of the water. He placed his oars in, straightened his legs and arms, while leaning forward. As he completed the first leg drive, John lowered his shoulder blades, with his back toward the bow of the boat, bent his elbows, and pulled the oars to his chest at the drive phase. Continuing to push the oar handle down until the blade just surfaced at the extraction stroke, John quickly rotated the oar ninety degrees so that the blade was parallel to the water. The recovery phase was now reached, and he leaned back, extended his legs, and moved his hands, clutching the oars close to his body, to begin at the catch position once more.

"To the right?" Mr. Stanhope called out from his position at the bow.

"Yes. There should be a flag a few yards ahead indicating the start."

"What the deuce? You were to wait for me!" a disgruntled voice declared from the shoreline.

John glanced over to see Mr. Thorne standing on the gravel pathway glaring at him, with his hands on his hips. Knowing he could not take his attention away from the strokes for more than a few seconds to argue with him, John shouted, "You were late. We will speak after the practice is over."

Chapter Three

"Place the chairs underneath the tree, close to the path, Jem," Aunt Prudence directed the groom. "Spread the blankets out close by and put the basket next to me. The other box in the cart is for you. Come back in an hour."

"I intend to read for a while before I eat, Mother." Abigail unbuttoned her spencer, removed her hat from her head, and sat down on a blanket, flipping a book open across her lap. "It is quite warm, even in the shade."

Ellen stood underneath the oak tree's large branches. She reached up to her chin to untie the lilac-hued silk ribbons on her bonnet, tossing it onto a nearby chair and closed her eyes with a sigh as a cool breeze suddenly blew off the water.

"Fanny did quite well when she advised which gowns would be of the most benefit to each of your proportions and countenances. You both look lovely. Take care and stay out of the sun," her aunt admonished as she settled herself onto a chair and reached into the container of food. "Gentlemen prefer a smooth, creamy complexion. Freckles would never do."

"Yes, Aunt." Ellen put a hand to her forehead to shield her eyes, and studied the river, looking for the boats. She soon spotted a craft carrying four men earnestly maneuvering their oars in and out of the water. She stood up on the balls of her feet. "Is it likely? Yes! I recognize him! Thomas is one of the rowing crew!"

"I can't believe it!" Abigail tossed her book down and stood up, shaking out the folds on the skirt of her sky-blue walking gown. "He hasn't been on a boat since he left Eton when he was eighteen!"

"How wonderfully expedient! Clever boy!" Aunt Prudence chuckled. She dropped her half-eaten, roasted chicken leg onto her plate, placed it on the seat next to her, and came to her feet. "Make certain you catch the gentlemen's gaze and wave your handkerchiefs at them, ladies!"

Abigail giggled as she walked across the blanket to stand next to Ellen. "It is highly unlikely they will find an opportunity to look away from the rowing course, Mother."

"Even so, if they should happen to glance this way, the gentlemen will be gratified if you respond in an animated manner to their notice. Where are they?"

Ellen pointed. "On the far side of the river. They are just now overtaking the other boat."

"I see. My goodness! Their craft is moving at quite a fast clip! Mr. Stanhope has the bow position. It is my understanding that spot is reserved for the strongest man on the crew," her aunt observed, with a keen glance at Ellen.

"Not necessarily. I am certain rowing requires every crew member to be stalwart as well as dependable." Ellen frowned. "I wonder what happened to the other gentleman?"

Abigail shrugged her shoulders and returned to her spot on the blanket. "Perhaps he felt ill this morning or possibly there was an important summons from his family asking him to return home."

"Regardless, Thomas appears to have occupied the vacant spot quite competently," Aunt Prudence observed with a smug expression. She returned to her chair.

Ellen concentrated her gaze on the boats. "I believe they won that race. They are coming back around and lining up at the start position with another craft alongside."

"Since the gentlemen's attentions are temporarily riveted on something other than yourselves, you should take the opportunity to have something to eat, my dears. As I mentioned earlier, a flawless, untarnished skin tone is much admired. It would also never do to have your complexions become sallow or dull from lack of sustenance."

Abigail grimaced. "Please stop this, Mother! I understand you wish for us to cultivate eligible connections, but is unseemly for Ellen and me to continually throw ourselves in the path of Mr. Stanhope and Mr. Rudder in order to gain their notice."

Aunt Prudence chuckled. "I am not suggesting anything of the sort! It is obvious the gentlemen have favored you both with noteworthy distinction. I am merely pointing out the advantages of promoting that achievement by presenting yourselves to them with the most favorable outward aspect and composure."

"I believe I will have some bread and cheese," Ellen remarked as she bent over the container of food, choosing to ignore her aunt's comments and outlandish eccentricity. "May I bring you something, Abigail?"

"Yes, thank you. A piece of chicken and some bread."

"Please pour me a glass of lemonade, Ellen." Aunt Prudence wiped her mouth with her handkerchief. "I bought a jug of ale and had Cook make a game pie for the gentlemen, if they should stop here after the race."

Abigail snorted. "No matter how charmed they may be by myself and my cousin, I doubt they will have the occasion to join us. Remember, after competing in the practice races, they must also return their equipment to the boathouse."

"We shall see. In the meantime, we should determine what events would be most suitable for Mr. Rudder and Mr. Stanhope to attend while they are in Bristol. It is imperative they come to the assembly rooms on Tuesday evening. I believe they would never turn down an opportunity to dance the cotillion and quadrille, even in our humble quarters. Attending balls is a well-established form of entertainment for gentlemen primarily residing in London," Aunt Prudence continued, undaunted by their lack of enthusiasm for her scheme.

Ellen handed the morsels of food to her cousin and the glass of lemonade to her aunt before taking a seat. She admitted to herself that she would like to know more of Mr. Rudder. They had both been at the Horsham House gathering, participated in outdoor activities, eaten meals at the same times, even danced together at the impromptu ball Lady Collins organized shortly before everyone returned home. Somehow, there had never been a chance to have a serious discussion together. She exchanged a few words with him at Camille's wedding in March. Regardless of her own wishes, it was incumbent upon her to remind Aunt Prudence of the tangible reason the gentlemen were in town. "We must not overlook the crew's daily race practice requirements. It is doubtful they will be at liberty to participate in many other diversions."

"Nonsense! There will be plenty of opportunity each day for them to enjoy concerts, attend the theatre and go on picnics if we sustain the warm weather we are currently enjoying. Do either of you have notions for other amusements?"

Ellen bit into a piece of cheese, chewed and swallowed it. "Recall last year, we planned to see the Triumphal Arch and the Black Castle? It rained the last four days of my visit, and our excursion had to be cancelled. If the weather continues fine, may we travel there?"

Aunt Prudence lowered her brows and studied her. "I am aware of your interest in architecture, Ellen. Is it wise to flaunt your enthusiasm for the subject to the gentlemen? It is not considered to be a customary diversion for young ladies of genteel upbringing."

"I disagree, Mother. An excellent notion!" Abigail stood up and walked over to the food box to pour herself a glass of lemonade. "There is no need to reference Ellen's indecorous interest in the construction of buildings. We can style the jaunt as something of interest to Mr. Stanhope and Mr. Rudder. To us, the trip will merely be an amusing diversion."

Ellen frowned as she recalled Mr. Stanhope's gentle reproaches to her singular pursuit the day before. "Mother and Father have always encouraged my absorption with architecture."

"Naturally. You are an only child." Aunt Prudence reached across the chair to pat her arm. "It is admirable your parents nurtured your curiosity when you were growing up. I am certain they would agree it is past time to dispense with these irregular sentiments. You need to begin to concentrate on preparing yourself to manage a family and a house of your own."

"Are you trying to say I am a bluestocking, Aunt?"

"Certainly, many would believe so."

"I have no talent for drawing and am unable to carry a tune. My embroidery and my play on the pianoforte are passable at best. Studying architecture and building structure has always brought me pleasure. I don't intend to plan or construct a dwelling."

"Of course not!" Abigail agreed. "I believe there is no shame in being labeled a bluestocking. My excessive preoccupation with reading makes me one. I say we take the excursion and simply enjoy ourselves. If nothing else, it gives Ellen and me an opportunity to learn more of Mr. Stanhope and Mr. Rudder. Surely you concur, Mother?"

"The outing would provide us with a perfect excuse to monopolize the gentlemen for several hours," she acknowledged, thoughtfully tapping her chin with one finger. "Although it is no more than a few miles away, a coach needs to be hired to convey us to the site. Perhaps the others will prefer to ride there."

"If they join us later today, I will inquire if they wish to accompany our party to visit the arch and castle." Abigail dropped her book into her lap and stretched her neck, staring at the water. "Do you think the practice has finished?"

Ellen stood up, reaching for her bonnet. "I believe I will walk a short way in that direction to see if I can determine if they are returning their boat to the dock."

"Don't go too far," her aunt advised. "We want you composed and reclining languidly against a chair when the gentlemen arrive."

Ellen disregarded her implication. "I will take a few steps near the river and promise to return in a few minutes. Do you wish to come with me, Abigail?"

"No, thank you. I want to reread a few lines of poetry I found particularly diverting."

"I will be back soon." Ellen tied the strings on her bonnet and walked out of the shaded meadow toward the water. She rounded the corner and took no more than twenty steps on the pathway when she spied someone standing on the riverbank just ahead of her.

"Cabbage head! He has no business being on that boat," the man growled and pointed one shaking finger at the river. "The other gent shouldn't be in the stroke position, either. That spot was meant for me."

Ellen studied the gentleman. He was tall and lanky, his upper body noticeably scrawny as the sleeves of his coat fluttered loosely across his arms in the breeze. In contrast to his height, he had a small, round head. His fine, almost translucent brown locks were brushed flat and forward across his forehead, with one unruly curl sticking up in the center of his scalp. A few gaunt strands of hair dangled over his thick brows and a dusting of coarse whiskers framed the side of his face, beginning below his ears and stretching down to a spot above his chin. A wide, red-hued nose dominated his face, his lips thin and stretched tight across a mouth in a grimacing expression, his eyes half-closed and squinting.

"I imagine there is a perfectly rational explanation for the situation. Perhaps you arrived late at the boathouse, which is why my cousin has taken your place," Ellen countered.

He turned his head and glared at her. "I'm not surprised that scoundrel is related to you. When I want

31

your opinion, I will ask for it."

Taken aback by the man's abhorrent, churlish manner, Ellen pivoted away from him and swiftly walked toward the dense woods bordering the quay, forgetting the promise she had made to her aunt.

Chapter Four

"I spotted the ladies on the shore near the starting line," Mr. Pratt commented after they spoke with Mr. Burke and returned the boat and oars to the boathouse. "My mother mentioned providing ale and a partridge pie for us to consume after the practice. She urged me to extend an invitation to all of you."

"I am decidedly parched and hungry. I gratefully accept," Mr. Stanhope answered.

"How can I refuse food and drink coupled with the delightful prospect of rapport with the ladies?" John grinned. "I welcome your proposal."

"Wonderful!" Mr. Pratt turned around. "Are you going to join us, Mr. Campbell?"

"No. No, thank you." He reached up to tug at his dangling neckcloth. "I should discover Mr. Thorne's whereabouts."

John frowned at him. "Make certain Mr. Thorne is aware it is imperative he meets us here tomorrow at ten o'clock. If he does not arrive on time, we will restore Mr. Pratt to a permanent position on our crew."

Mr. Campbell pursed his lips and nodded. "I understand. I will speak with him."

Mr. Stanhope studied his retreating form. "What are the chances Mr. Thorne is late again tomorrow?"

John grunted. "If you wish to make a wager on the possibility, I will say you have a good prospect of winning."

Mr. Pratt took off his hat and wiped his forehead with his handkerchief. "I am grateful for your confidence in my ability to row, after my doubtful performance today."

"A ridiculous notion!" Mr. Stanhope gave him a teasing jab on the arm. "After so many years of not participating in races, you did wonderfully. It was only a matter of accommodating the timing. You quickly came around."

"I agree. You did quite well." John reached inside his coat pocket and pulled out the tin. "Anyone for a clove comfit?"

"No. Thank you." Mr. Stanhope turned to Mr. Pratt. "I never heard of a comfit until Mr. Rudder explained them to me this morning. They are pieces of spices compressed into a ball."

Mr. Pratt raised his brows. "Interesting, but I believe I will pass on your offer, Mr. Rudder."

John popped one into his mouth, shut the lid, and returned the container to his pocket. "Lead the way to the refreshments, young man."

The gentlemen strolled along a graveled pathway bordering the New Cut portion of the river. Once they reached the spot opposite the race starting line, John noticed a rocky knoll, bordered by a dense stand of ash trees. A few more steps brought them to a flat, grassy field shaded by several large oaks. Mrs. and Miss Pratt were standing together in front of a group of chairs.

Mrs. Pratt turned to face them when they walked into the clearing.

"Oh! Thank goodness you have come!" She gripped her handkerchief with shaking hands. Miss Pratt reached out to touch her mother's arm.

"What is wrong?" Mr. Pratt ran up to them.

"It's Ellen, Miss Cather." Miss Pratt paused and took a deep breath. "She left us nearly an hour ago, intending to walk a short distance near the water to discover if your craft was returning to the dock. She pledged to stay close by and return immediately. I was reading and Mother was busy reorganizing the food box, so it took a while before we comprehended Miss Cather had not come back. We have asked Jem, our groom, to search the surrounding area for her."

Mr. Stanhope frowned. "She is a young, defenseless woman. Surely, she would not wander off by herself?"

"No, she has much more sense," John noted staunchly. "Which means she cannot have gone far."

"Perhaps she came upon an acquaintance from London and stopped to speak with them?" Mr. Pratt suggested.

"Don't be absurd, Thomas!" his mother scolded as she wiped at the tears on her cheeks. "If that had been the case, Ellen would have escorted her friends here and presented them to us."

"Does Miss Cather know how to swim?" Mr. Stanhope shaded his eyes with one hand to his forehead as he stared at the river.

John grunted. The thought of her drowning hit him like a direct punch to his stomach. He hastily swallowed some fresh air. "I believe the ladies have suffered enough anguish without making such rash statements. We are accomplishing nothing by standing here speculating on what has happened. I intend to search the woods behind us. Mr. Stanhope, I suggest you take the path along the river."

"I will stay here with Mother and Abigail," Mr. Pratt declared. "I will shout if Ellen should appear."

"Very good." John turned and sprinted up and over the knoll and down the other side. With a few long strides, he found himself on the edge of a dense canopy of ash trees. "Miss Cather! Ellen!"

He contemplated the rough ground in front of him, looking for an imprint of a lady's slipper. Since it was early spring, only a few leaves were scattered on the ground. He quickly comprehended the motion of the edge of a woman's gown or the bottom of her shoe across the surface wouldn't leave enough of an impression to provide him with a clue to her movements or location. He took several steps deeper into the woods. "Miss Cather!"

"I am here!"

The sound of her voice brought a sudden, intense sensation of relief. The pounding at his temples ceased and he experienced an abrupt, lightheaded response that almost brought him to his knees. He took a sustaining breath and made his way forward. He found himself in an open meadow. He glanced to the right and to the left.

"Look up."

He gazed at the branches of a nearby tree and jumped. Not literally, but what he observed certainly made him flinch, and his heart skipped a beat. Emerging from underneath the bottom edge of a lilac-colored gown were two well-turned ankles attached to a pair of dainty feet. They dangled from a spot just above the top of his head. He moved closer, taking pleasure in the delightful image for a few seconds before asking, "Do you often climb trees as a source of amusement, Miss Cather?"

She huffed and adjusted the arm she had wrapped

around the tree trunk. "There is no need for you to poke fun at my predicament, Mr. Rudder. I stepped into the woods for a moment and heard a wailing noise. I walked toward the sound and discovered this tiny kitten stuck in the branches."

"It is not my intention to make you an object of ridicule." For the first time since he spotted her, John noticed the gray-and-black kitten perched on the front edge of her gown. "Please, continue your explanation."

She reached out with her free hand to rub the animal's back. "Because of the low-lying, bottom branch, it was an easy matter to make my way up the tree. However, the little scamp evaded my initial attempts to capture him. My slippers fell from my feet during the struggle. I managed to grab the kitten just before he leaped to a higher branch. Upon securing him and looking down, I found the contemplation of returning to the ground much more daunting than it was going up."

"You do realize the mother cat is probably not far away? It shouldn't be too long before she notices one of her offspring is missing and returns to collect the reprobate?"

The words barely left his mouth when a streak of white, fluffy fur leaped across his shoes and dashed up the trunk of the tree. Giving first an ear-splitting meow, the cat plucked the kitten from Miss Cather's lap and bounded to the ground with the animal's scruff tucked safely in its mouth. They disappeared down a pathway into the forest.

He studied Miss Cather, noting with pleasure, her flushed, rosy cheeks. "That worry has successfully resolved itself. Now, what do you propose we accomplish first? Your aunt, cousins, and Mr. Stanhope are quite concerned over your location and safety. The groom has been dispatched to search for you. Should I inform them I have discovered your location and then return to assist you to the ground?"

One hand tightly gripping the trunk, Miss Cather reached up with the other to clutch a lock of hair in her fingers that had escaped from its moorings. She tucked the strand back under the crown of her bonnet and sighed. "I would prefer that you didn't leave me suspended here any longer. How are we to manage my removal?"

He grinned, relishing the momentary, unique position he found himself in as her defender and protector. "Scoot forward to the edge of the limb. Continue bracing yourself with one hand around the trunk. When you are ready, let go and drop into my arms."

"Drop into…? I couldn't!"

"I assure you, Miss Cather, I will catch you with ease. The branch you are sitting on is not too great a distance above the top of my head. What is wrong? Are you afraid to jump?"

She scowled down at him. "I do not fear for my own safety. Rather, I worry that I will cause you an injury."

"Have you located her? Miss Cather! Whatever are you doing up in that tree? Goodness gracious! You have lost your slippers!" Mr. Stanhope gasped as he came to a sudden stop a few feet away.

"We will discuss the reason for her awkward location and the circumstances momentarily. Please go inform the others she has been found safe."

Mr. Stanhope ignored his request, continuing to

gawk at her. "Are you certain? Do you need my assistance, Mr. Rudder?"

"No. I do not. Be on your way." John turned back to deal with the business at hand. He smiled up at Miss Cather, spreading his arms wide. "Well?"

She cast a furtive glance at Mr. Stanhope, who made a huffing sound with his nose, before turning and marching back toward the clearing. Miss Cather shifted her position and gazed directly down at him. "I trust you."

With that sincere declaration, she wiggled forward on the branch, and loosened her tight grip on the tree, giving the trunk a hearty shove with her gloved hand, while simultaneously leaning toward him.

"Umph!" The sudden impact of her torso against his chest momentarily robbed him of his breath. He quickly adjusted his stance, wrapping one arm around her waist and the other under her knees. "I-I have you!"

Miss Cather struggled in his arms. He tightened his grip, and he felt her relax. She bent forward, reclining against him, wrapping her hands around his neck. She sighed and peeked up at him through her long lashes. "Thank you. I apologize for not thinking clearly and creating this mortifying incident."

The strings on her bonnet had become loose and her hat tipped backward, sliding off her head, revealing her unimpaired countenance to his fascinated gaze. A tantalizing whiff of lavender combined with orange blossom rose from her hair. He took a moment to relish the fragrance before replying, "There is absolutely no need to express remorse. I am happy to have been of service."

"That aroma." She sniffed the air. "It reminds me of

a cinnamon-and-clove tart my nanny would make for me when I was a little girl."

"I believe you are smelling my clove comfits." He slowly lowered her to the ground. "Once your slippers are on, I'll let you try one."

"Oh! I am sorry!" She hastily stepped away from him and thrust her feet into her shoes, while reaching up with trembling hands to secure the bonnet.

"Again, there is no need to apologize." He grinned as he noted her creamy, soft cheeks turning rosy once more. "You required a moment to compose yourself after dropping out of a tree. It is quite understandable."

"I am grateful for your quick comprehension of my embarrassing predicament." She sighed and finished tying the bonnet strings, giving the brim of her hat a hasty tug. "I must assure my aunt and cousins of my safety."

"Wait one moment. I promised you a comfit." He reached into his pocket for the tin and opened the lid, offering it to her. "They are bits of clove mashed and pressed together."

She studied the contents intently for a moment before reaching inside the container and choosing one of the smaller chunks. "Do I chew it?"

"I would recommend sucking on it. I find the taste especially refreshing after a heavy meal."

She carefully placed the comfit on her tongue. Her eyes widened. "Delightful!"

He chuckled at her guileless response. "I am happy you like them. I must admit I have formed a tendency to pop one in my mouth several times a day."

"Where do you obtain them?" She frowned. "They aren't made in our country?"

"I believe they can be purchased in the shops that carry imported goods from India. My uncle works for the East India Company. He brought several tins back with him a few months ago. Shall we join the others?" He offered her his arm. They began to make their way through the trees toward the water and the pathway bordering the quay. A sudden recollection made him stop. "I just recalled something you said. *I stepped into the woods for a moment...* I understood you left your aunt and cousin to determine if we had returned to the dock. Why did you come here?"

Chapter Five

Ellen cast a glance at the path leading out of the clearing before turning back to Mr. Rudder. "I had an unpleasant encounter with the fourth member of your crew."

"Mr. Thorne? What occurred?"

She pretended to study the ground, avoiding his piercing look. "He was standing on the bank just above the water as I came around the corner from our picnic location. He pointed at your boat and made belligerent comments regarding Thomas taking his spot and you occupying his rightful position."

"Go on."

"His imprudent statements and brazen assumptions annoyed me. I spoke out before I thought better of doing so and informed him that I believed he had most probably forfeited his place to my cousin because he had arrived late at the boathouse. His manner became quite gruff and surly. He bellowed an indignant pronouncement, advising me he had no interest in my opinion and wasn't surprised I was related to the man who had replaced him." She sighed. "His repellent demeanor unsettled and flustered me. I immediately turned away and strode into the woods, knowing only the urgent need to escape him."

Mr. Rudder frowned as he clasped her arm with his free hand. "I apologize for Mr. Thorne's conduct. His behavior has been a disappointment and a great source of frustration from shortly after our initial meeting at the tavern. I am becoming worried he spends most of his days and nights drinking heavily."

"It is my conjecture…" She paused at the sound of footsteps.

Mr. Rudder bent toward her and whispered in her ear. "Don't mention Mr. Thorne to the others. I will discuss what took place separately with Mr. Pratt and Mr. Stanhope later."

"Ellen! Mother and I were beside ourselves with worry."

She turned away from Mr. Rudder to observe Abigail making her way down the side of the knoll. Mr. Stanhope shadowed her cousin, offering her his arm when she encountered a patch of rocky, uneven ground at the bottom of the ridge.

"I am well. I apologize for causing everyone needless distress." She glanced at Mr. Rudder. "Perhaps we should join my aunt and Thomas before I explain?"

"Yes, I agree. It would make better sense to relate your account of the circumstances all at once."

Mr. Stanhope released Abigail's arm and strode up to Ellen. "Are you certain you shouldn't immediately return to your aunt's abode? I have no doubt you require a moment's reflection as well as a sustaining cup of tea."

"Reflection?" She frowned at him. "To what are you referring?"

"Certainly, you understand, Miss Cather, you have come dangerously close to crossing the line of what is acceptable for young, unmarried ladies?" he sputtered. "Going off alone, without a maid in attendance, is an open invitation for rogues and other unsavory characters to approach you."

Ellen felt a rush of heat on her cheeks as she inwardly acknowledged the truth of his sentiments, given what had occurred. She quickly came up with a plausible excuse for her cousin to hear, knowing Mr. Stanhope would learn the real reason she sought refuge in the woods later from Mr. Rudder. "I thought to step under the shade of the trees for a brief period to cool myself. When I heard the kitten's cries of distress and noted his position, haphazardly dangling from a limb, you cannot think to chastise me for my well-meaning intentions."

"A kitten!" Abigail sighed deeply and her brown eyes widened as she looked to the right and then the left. "Where is he?"

"The mother cat snatched him from Miss Cather's lap a few minutes ago," Mr. Rudder informed her with a grin. "They disappeared into the woods. Shall we join the others?"

Abigail wrapped one gloved hand around Ellen's arm as they made their way back over the knoll and down the other side to the path. "I wish I had seen the sweet kitten. What color was he?"

Ellen smiled as she recalled holding the silky-smooth animal in her lap. "His tiny body was a light gray hue. His ears and the tip of his tail were darker, almost black."

"Oh, how adorable!"

"Ellen! Thank goodness you are not injured!" Aunt Prudence rushed toward them as they walked into the clearing. "I was beside myself with worry."

"I am unharmed, Aunt. As I explained to Abigail, I walked into the wood seeking a moment in the shade and heard a kitten crying. I spotted him perched upon a tree limb not too far above me. I was able to climb up and secure the tiny animal just before the mother cat appeared and plucked him from my lap. I will need to purchase a new pair of gloves." She held up one hand to show a tear in the material across her palm. "The bark was quite rough in a few places."

"Goodness me!" her aunt gasped and reached out to clutch her arm. "Come, sit down and have a glass of lemonade."

Ellen kept silent as she followed her aunt to the group of chairs. She secured the seat she had taken earlier underneath the large oak tree. Abigail sat on the blanket once again.

Mr. Stanhope came to stand next to Ellen. He bent toward her, speaking softly. "Miss Cather, are you certain you would not prefer to compose yourself at your aunt's home? I will gladly escort you and the other ladies there."

"There is absolutely no need for you to do so, Mr. Stanhope." She swallowed the frustration she felt over his persistent cossetting and moderated the harsh tone in her voice. "I am well and wish to repose here in the shade by the water."

"I am quite happy to know you wish to stay, Ellen." Her aunt turned away as the groom walked into the clearing. "As you can see, Jem, Miss Cather has been found. Please return in thirty minutes."

"Very good, ma'am."

Aunt Prudence bent over the box of food, filling a glass with lemonade. She handed it to Ellen and then waved the gentlemen over. "Please join us. Thomas will pour you some ale. There is a partridge pie, if you are hungry."

"I can't recall the last time we climbed trees together, Cousin," Thomas said with a chuckle as he bent over the box and picked up the jug. "I wasn't aware you continued to partake in the endeavor."

Ellen sipped her lemonade before replying. "Only when something as enticing as a kitten catches my interest."

"Ha! It is to be hoped you don't see too many of the furry little animals lurking on high branches for the rest of your stay in Bristol then." Thomas handed full tankards of ale to Mr. Stanhope and Mr. Rudder. "If you were to become stuck again, a fortuitous opportunity to be rescued might not be possible as it was today."

Ellen wrinkled her nose at him. "I will take note of your sensible admonition, Thomas."

"There is a good chance you will come upon other errant animals. It is springtime, after all." Aunt Prudence giggled. "Mr. Stanhope, take a seat next to my niece. I will dish you up a piece of partridge pie and some morsels of cheese. You must be ravenous."

"I would enjoy sampling the pie. Thank you, Mrs. Pratt." Mr. Stanhope sat down on the chair she indicated and took a sip of ale, placing the tankard at his feet when she handed him a full plate.

Aunt Prudence turned to the others. "I am sorry. I brought only three chairs. Thomas, you may sit on the tree stump over there. Abigail, scoot over so that Mr. Rudder may join you on the blanket."

Ellen winced with embarrassment as she observed her aunt's obvious ploy to orchestrate the two gentlemen's positions. She came to her feet. "Mr. Rudder may have my seat. I will sit with Abigail."

"Don't be absurd, Ellen," her aunt quickly admonished. "You stay put and compose yourself. I will see everyone has something to eat. Then we will discuss our notions for excursions and amusements in the coming days."

"I will gladly join Miss Pratt." Mr. Rudder reached out for his plate of food and took a place on the edge of the blanket.

Ellen sat down once again with a sigh.

"You are not hungry, Miss Cather?" Mr. Stanhope inquired between mouthfuls of pie.

She shook her head. "I had bread and cheese earlier."

"I am not surprised your appetite has deserted you." Mr. Stanhope placed his half-empty plate at his feet and picked up the tankard. He took a sip from it. "The events that transpired this morning have doubtless left you with sensations of agitation and disquiet."

Ellen opened her mouth intending to fervently deny experiencing anything like those emotions, when she thought better of it. Obviously, Mr. Stanhope believed only one type of reaction was possible for a gently reared lady to have, and there would be no possibility of convincing him otherwise.

"Did you have a chance to read any of the poems, Miss Pratt?" Mr. Rudder questioned.

"Yes, I did. I brought the volume of Wordsworth poetry with me today." She picked the book up from nearby on the blanket, holding it aloft. "I found the poem you referred to, Mr. Rudder. It is lovely! I especially enjoyed the image of the daffodils *tossing their heads in a sprightly dance*. Are you aware it is also called *I Wandered Lonely as a Cloud*?"

"I am." Mr. Rudder smiled at her. "I prefer to call the poem by the flower name since it conjures up such wonderful images of daffodils in my mind. Wordsworth's comparisons are glorious as well. *'Continuous as the stars that shine and twinkle on the Milky Way, They stretched in never-ending line along the margin of a bay...'* It is quite apparent why that memory brought him great joy."

"What notions had you ladies come up with for our entertainment?" Thomas asked, obviously bored with the topics of poetry and flowers.

"My cousin had a suggestion for an excursion. If you gentlemen are free tomorrow afternoon, we thought it would be amusing to visit the Triumphal Arch and Black Castle," Abigail announced.

"Triumphal Arch. Isn't that the place you wished to explore last year, Ellen?" Thomas reached for the plate of food his mother handed to him.

"Yes, it is. Recall we had heavy rain the last few days of my stay. There was never a chance to visit."

"Of what interest is this place to you, Miss Cather?" Mr. Stanhope queried.

She opened her mouth to describe the captivating carvings set inside the niches on each side of the arch as well as the compelling architectural elements on the formation, but then she paused, remembering the ladies' words of admonishment relating to expressing overt interest in the design and function of structures. Inwardly sighing with frustration, while at the same time acknowledging the validity of their assertions, she answered with a shrug of her shoulders, "There is no prevalent appeal, it is simply an excuse to take a short journey out of the confines of the city."

He frowned. "As Mrs. Pratt reminded us, it is springtime. Would not a short trip to view wildflowers growing in the lush, green fields be of more pleasure to you? Perhaps we might even come upon a mound of bluebells!"

"Indeed!" She forced her lips into the shape of a smile. "Or a more stupendous occurrence, and surely of immense gratification to my cousin and Mr. Rudder, would be to stumble across a meadow of daffodils."

"Considering it is the middle of April, there might be a favorable opportunity to accomplish both in one excursion," Thomas disclosed, tapping one finger against his chin. "I recall Arnos Vale is known for its grand display of bluebells from April to early May. The field is quite near the arch."

"A stupendous notion, brother!" Abigail clasped her gloved hands together and gave him a warm smile.

"Nothing could be better! I had no inkling you could be so ingenious, Thomas." Aunt Prudence chuckled, while studying her son with raised brows.

"Now that we have settled upon a destination, we must decide how best to be transported there." Mr. Rudder stood up from the blanket and took his empty plate over to the box.

"Put the plate there, on top of my dish," Aunt Prudence advised him. "If you gentlemen would care to ride, we ladies can obtain a carriage. Our family has always used the services of Mr. Finch and Sons near Temple Gate whenever we require mounts or vehicles for a short time period."

"I will take care of securing our modes of transport, Mother," Thomas offered.

"Shall we settle on a time and a location to

assemble?" Mr. Stanhope inquired, with a glance at Mr. Rudder. "Perhaps at noon? That will give us time to return the boat and don a change of clothing."

"We can meet at Mr. Finch's stables. He is located just off the Bath Road, which is the route we take to the arch," Thomas suggested.

"Does this plan meet with everyone's approval?" Aunt Prudence asked.

"I will gladly join the expedition," Mr. Rudder answered, as he walked back toward Abigail, who was balancing her glass in one hand, struggling to stand from the blanket. He offered her his arm. "Let me assist you, Miss Pratt."

"I plan to join in the excursion as well." Mr. Stanhope came to his feet and placed his empty plate on top of the stack of other used dishes.

The groom strode into the clearing at that moment.

"Jem. We are finished. Gather the box, chairs, and blankets, place the things in the cart, and return to our residence. The ladies and I will walk home."

Mr. Stanhope turned after depositing his plate, walking with intent back toward Ellen. He came to a stop in front of her. "Come, Miss Cather, take my arm. I will see that you get back unscathed."

"But…?" She slowly stood, gazing intently at her aunt with a silent plea.

"I am much obliged to you, Mr. Stanhope," Aunt Prudence gushed with a warm smile for him, ignoring Ellen's unspoken appeal. "Abigail and I will follow right behind you. No doubt my niece is still feeling a trifle out of sorts after her ordeal."

Ellen pursed her lips together, putting a shaking hand on Mr. Stanhope's arm. How much she disliked not having the ability to decide where she went and who she went with for herself! Mr. Stanhope led her out of the clearing. Just before they rounded the corner and stepped onto the walkway, Ellen twisted around and glanced over her shoulder. She got a glimpse of Mr. Rudder's wavy brown hair as he bent over the book of poetry Abigail was brandishing in front of him.

"You will feel much better once you are back inside your aunt's home. I would advise you to request the housekeeper to brew you a tisane with chamomile to reduce the anxiety you are no doubt experiencing. Additionally, a cold compress could help. A few minutes with the cloth placed upon your forehead while you recline in a comfortable chair, would be most beneficial to soothe your disordered emotions." Mr. Stanhope patted her hand that rested on the sleeve of his coat.

Ellen did not answer him. Nothing came to mind, other than something harsh or insulting.

"Wait! Miss Pratt has a brilliant suggestion," Mr. Rudder called out to them.

Mr. Stanhope paused on the edge of the pathway. "I can't imagine…"

Ellen tugged on his arm. "I would like to hear what my cousin has to say."

He sighed. "Very well."

They turned around and strolled back to the others. Abigail stood on the fringe of the blanket, smiling. Mr. Rudder hovered at her side.

"Repeat what you said to me a moment ago, Miss Pratt," Mr. Rudder prompted.

"Knowing my cousin as well as I do, I could not imagine her wishing to sit inside on such a lovely, warm day. I alluded to the possibility of all of us going for a short boat ride." Abigail blushed and turned to Mr. Rudder. "If it would not inconvenience the gentlemen by returning to the water so soon after the race practice."

He chuckled. "I would enjoy it. However, I believe it is most important to ascertain Miss Cather's wishes."

Ellen released Mr. Stanhope's arm and strode forward to Abigail's side. "What a lovely notion!"

Mr. Stanhope took a few steps toward Ellen. He frowned at her. "I have just finished advising Miss Cather of the best methods to reduce any lingering sensations of apprehension. I am certain peace, quiet, and rest in her aunt's comforting abode would be the best remedy after her recent turmoil."

"Let's ask the lady herself what her preference is," Mr. Rudder declared. "Miss Cather, do you wish to return home, or would you like to take a boat around the Floating Harbor?"

Ellen smiled at him. "An excursion on the water sounds enchanting. What type of craft do you suggest we use?"

"You cannot mean to take the ladies out in racing boats?" Mr. Stanhope asked as he reached into his waistcoat pocket to pull out his handkerchief with a shaking hand.

"No, not at all. Recall Mr. Burke pointed out the wherries that were stored in the boathouse? It should be a simple matter to ask him if we can take one out," Mr. Rudder replied.

"A wherry?" Aunt Prudence's brows rose on her forehead. "I believe I took such a boat across the Thames to Vauxhall Gardens when I was a young lady."

"You are correct, Mother," Thomas answered. "Wherries were commonly used for that purpose."

"I understand there are currently more wherries on the Thames near London than there are hackney carriages in the city," Mr. Rudder clarified. "What do you say to Miss Pratt's proposition, Mrs. Pratt, Mr. Pratt?"

Aunt Prudence contemplated Ellen, as she stood close to Mr. Stanhope, and then she considered Abigail in her position near Mr. Rudder. "I believe my daughter's notion is quite expedient. The weather is perfect for such an excursion as well."

Thomas chuckled before commenting, "I gladly agree to participate in the proposed jaunt. Once we secure the wherry from Mr. Burke, is it advisable to sail it here to pick up the ladies?"

Mr. Rudder frowned as he turned to stare at the water. "That would involve sailing back through the more turbulent waters of the New Cut. I suggest the ladies walk with us to the docks on the Floating Harbor near the boathouse. We will conduct our business with Mr. Burke, and then carry the craft over. What is your opinion, Mr. Stanhope?"

He sighed as he patted both of his cheeks with his handkerchief before tucking the piece of linen back into his waistcoat pocket. "I concur, Mr. Rudder. It would be inadvisable to subject the ladies to the rigors of the strong currents found inside the New Cut."

"I think it would be best if I accompany them to the dock," Thomas added. "Once you arrive with the boat, I will provide them boarding assistance."

"Excellent. Mrs. Pratt, your groom will see to the transport of the rest of your belongings?" Mr. Rudder inquired.

"Certainly." She turned toward the spot where the

cart was parked. "Here is my groom. Jem, please see that everything is packed up and returned to the house."

"Yes, ma'am."

"Here, Jem." Abigail handed him her book of poetry. "Please give this to my maid."

"Very good, Miss Pratt."

"We are free to leave then." Mr. Rudder stepped forward and offered his arm to Mrs. Pratt.

At the same time, Ellen reached for Abigail's hand.

"Thank you, Mr. Rudder. I am certain Thomas can…" Aunt Prudence stopped speaking to stare at Ellen. "Very well."

Ellen met her aunt's look with an impassive countenance. "Walk with me, dear cousin."

"Of course. A moment." Abigail finished tying the ribbons on her hat into a bow underneath her chin before putting her hand on Ellen's sleeve.

"I wished to express my prodigious appreciation to you for coming up with the grand notion of taking a boat journey," Ellen whispered as they advanced onto the pathway.

"A pleasure." Abigail frowned. "I trust Mr. Stanhope is not affronted by my presumption. I am certain he comports himself with the best intentions."

Ellen risked a glance from the corner of her eye at Thomas and Mr. Stanhope as the two men strolled behind them. She heard the words "boat" and "crew" and deduced they were deep in discussion concerning the regatta. Ellen bent forward to speak softly into Abigail's ear. "Mr. Stanhope appears to believe all women are frail, helpless creatures."

"Surely not!" Abigail pursed her lips together, staring at the ground as they walked. "I imagine he sees himself as a staunch defender, a person who can provide clarity in a situation where sensitive, impressionable ladies might require the benefit of his understanding."

"How noble of you, cousin." Ellen giggled as she squeezed Abigail's arm. "You have aptly justified Mr. Stanhope's exceptional, and in my case, often exasperating stance."

Mr. Rudder came to a halt near the entrance to Prince Bridge while speaking in an undertone to Ellen's aunt. She nodded her head in apparent agreement with what he said before he turned to face the rest of their group, "Mr. Pratt, please take over as escort for the ladies. Cross here and make your way to Teast's Dock. Mr. Stanhope and I will secure the wherry from Mr. Burke and meet you there."

"Very good." Thomas stepped forward and held out his arm. "Come, Mother. Follow close behind, Abigail and Ellen."

Without speaking, Mr. Stanhope glanced at Ellen before he swiveled around and trailed Mr. Rudder down the hill toward Bathurst Basin and the shipyards.

Ellen frowned as she studied their retreating figures. A gentle tug on her arm brought her back to the present.

"Mother and Thomas are already several yards ahead of us," Abigail admonished. "We must hurry."

"Oh, yes." Ellen turned and strode forward with her cousin at her side.

"Is something wrong?" Abigail inquired as they made their way across the bridge, taking long, extended strides.

Ellen took a deep breath before replying, "I am concerned that my disregard for Mr. Stanhope's anxieties over possible negative repercussions I might suffer after becoming stuck in the tree, indicates a narrow-minded, selfish demeanor. That was not my intention. I appreciate his advice, but I fear he doesn't fully comprehend my disposition. Nevertheless, I must apologize to him."

"Nonsense." Abigail slowed her pace as they neared the others. "I doubt he has taken offense. As I mentioned previously, Mr. Stanhope sees himself playing a certain role in distressing situations. Alternatively, you pride yourself on the ability to act independently. I imagine he might be confused by your refusal to follow his recommendations. Doubtless, he rarely encounters determined, strong-willed women."

Ellen chuckled as they walked up to Aunt Prudence and Thomas. "Most likely he has not. I still intend to speak with him to clarify my decision to take a turn on the water."

"We will wait for the gentlemen here," Thomas informed them, as he helped his mother climb the wooden stairs leading to the dock. "I'm not certain if they will arrive by water or will carry the boat to this location."

Ellen strolled to the edge of the dock to study the surrounding area. Usually, the weather was too poor to spend much time near the water on her visits. Several wooden barrels were lined up in rows on the quayside, as well as a few carts and a pile of fishing nets. A group of sailors gathered around a ramshackle building a few feet away. A man holding a long sheet of vellum stood in the doorway.

"That is the harbormaster's office. The dock workers collect their wages from him," Thomas explained.

"Quite intriguing." Ellen gazed at the crowd of men a moment more before she turned to smile at him. "You deduced my thoughts before I had a chance to form a query, Thomas."

He grinned. "It was a simple matter to predict once I observed your fixed interest."

"The gentlemen have arrived with the wherry," Aunt Prudence announced, pointing to the water.

Ellen pivoted to face the harbor. Mr. Stanhope and Mr. Rudder were sitting on separate benches inside a sleek, wooden boat. They dipped their oars into the water in unison as the craft neared the dock. A tall, skinny lad stood at the bow of the boat holding a coil of rope.

"Mr. Pratt!" Mr. Stanhope shouted. "Take the dock line from Horace and secure it before you help the ladies to board."

Horace tossed the line as the craft nudged the edge of the dock. Thomas caught the length of rope, swiftly tethering it to a nearby post, before turning to Aunt Prudence. "Mother, give me your hand."

"The lad will assist as well," Mr. Rudder declared from his position near the bow. "Mrs. Pratt and Miss Pratt, take the bench at the stern. Mr. Pratt and Miss Cather, you will sit on the seat in front of them."

With awkward, tottering steps, Aunt Prudence maneuvered her portly frame into the boat, and with both Thomas's and Horace's help, safely secured her seat. Within minutes, Abigail had taken her place next to her mother, and Ellen sat, facing away from them, on the bench next to Thomas.

"Cast us off, lad!" Mr. Stanhope ordered.

Horace untied the rope, tossing the dock line to Thomas, who coiled it into a neat bundle, and tucked it away underneath his seat.

As the wherry glided forward on the water, Ellen noted the assorted groups of people making their way down the bustling quayside thoroughfare. Mostly consisting of robust, sun-bronzed sailors, there were several clusters of ladies in light-colored, muslin walking gowns, promenading along the walkway with their children at their sides. The nannies, many displaying austere facial expressions, trailed closely behind their charges. As Ellen watched, two rambunctious boys suddenly pulled away from their mothers to chase a loose puppy.

Thomas pivoted on the bench next to Ellen. "Are you comfortable, Mother?"

"Yes, I am. A delightful experience!" She gazed straight ahead, toward the bow of the boat, with an impish grin curving her mouth. "Mr. Rudder, would you not agree my daughter's notion was quite prodigious?"

Mr. Rudder smiled at her as he bent forward to dip the oars in the water. "I can't think of a better way to spend a sunny afternoon, Mrs. Pratt."

Ellen wasn't paying much attention to their discussion. She was preoccupied watching the antics of the boys chasing the puppy. They scampered around several groups of sailors strolling along the quayside. She giggled as the dog suddenly burrowed underneath a fishing net, momentarily evading capture.

"I am assuaged by the sound of your laughter, Miss Cather," Mr. Stanhope murmured. "I applaud you for your valiant attempt to appear calm."

Ellen looked away from the bustling walkway to study him, her brows raised in surprise. "I do not understand. You recall, I was eager to join the excursion?"

"Yes, yes. I remember. Your achievement is quite admirable."

"Mr. Pratt, would you care to try your hand at rowing a wherry?" Mr. Rudder inquired. "Mr. Stanhope will keep the craft steady while we switch places. It is a simple matter in these calm waters."

With Mr. Stanhope's attention elsewhere, Ellen deliberated over the meaning of his cryptic comments. Unable to decipher the significance, she decided to question him later. Ellen turned to Mr. Rudder as he took the seat next to her.

"Are you enjoying yourself, Miss Cather?" He studied her. "You certainly appear cheerful and at ease."

"Oh, yes! The day is ending in quite a satisfying manner." Ellen frowned as she recalled her awkward position in the tree and Mr. Rudder's subsequent rescue earlier that morning. "I'm sorry. I have just realized I inadequately expressed my considerable appreciation for your timely assistance today. I can only excuse my negligence by admitting my acute sensations of shame and embarrassment at the time."

He grinned at her. "A pleasure, Miss Cather. I am gratified I discovered you shortly after you went missing and managed to extricate you with nothing more than a few, minor scratches."

"I am exceptionally grateful." Despite the fresh breeze coming off the water, Ellen felt her face growing hot as she gazed into Mr. Rudder's gleaming hazel eyes.

"We must do this again, Ellen, when you come visit us next year, if the weather is nice," Abigail observed.

Ellen looked away from Mr. Rudder and trained her gaze on Abigail. Oh, dear! What exactly had she spoken of? She recalled hearing something about "nice weather." "Yes, I agree. I don't remember it ever being this warm in April."

"There is one detail you are forgetting, ladies. Thomas could not skipper this craft by himself," Aunt Prudence gushed, with her brows raised.

"I am certain Mr. Burke could provide you with a couple of enterprising, young sailors like Horace to join the crew," Mr. Rudder pointed out. "I will speak with him on the subject when we return the boat."

"We are back where we started," Mr. Stanhope called. "Are we to drop our passengers off at the same dock?"

"One moment." Mr. Rudder smiled at Ellen, then Abigail, and finally, Aunt Prudence. "Would the ladies care to sail around the harbor one more time?"

Abigail looked at Ellen. "What do you wish to do?

Ellen glanced at Aunt Prudence before answering. She had turned away to face the water, but Ellen managed to detect her aunt raising her handkerchief in front of her mouth to stifle a yawn. The choice to make was obvious. "I am quite ready to return to shore. My thanks to all of you for a wonderful boat ride!"

"You're very welcome, Miss Cather," Mr. Rudder answered. He came to his feet and pointed toward the water. "There is a dock on the other side of the harbor, close to Queen's Square. Would that be more convenient, Mrs. Pratt?"

"Yes. Thank you."

As the wherry crossed the harbor to pull up at the opposite dock, Ellen observed Horace standing watching their progress from the quayside. It appeared he noted their alternate destination. He sprinted across a nearby bridge and raced forward just as the wherry touched the side of the dock.

"Good lad!" Mr. Rudder yelled as Thomas stood and tossed Horace the dock line.

With Horace's enthusiastic assistance, their boat was promptly tied and secured to the dock. Mr. Stanhope dropped his oars onto the deck, swiftly scampering out of the craft, before turning to help as they disembarked. He held his arm out to Abigail first.

Aunt Prudence slowly rose from her place on the bench. At that moment, a small wave splashed against the side of the boat, causing it to rock. She took a wobbly step forward. Mr. Rudder rushed up to her and placed one hand on her arm.

"Careful!"

She clutched his sleeve and gave him a wobbly smile. "I almost lost my balance. Thank you for coming to my rescue."

"A pleasure." He put his other hand at her back, guiding her forward until she reached Mr. Stanhope.

Mr. Rudder turned to Ellen and gave her his arm as she awkwardly stepped across the bench, catching the heel of her slipper on the edge of the seat. "I have you! I am happy you enjoyed yourself, Miss Cather. I will see you tomorrow afternoon."

"I look forward to it. Thank you again." She smiled at him and turned to grasp Mr. Stanhope's outstretched arm.

He guided her to the edge of the dock and continued to support her as they walked down the wooden stairs together. "It takes a few moments to regain your balance. There you are, safely on dry ground once more."

Ellen suddenly remembered her intention to explain

why she had chosen to go on the boat ride and to ask him to explain his earlier comments. "Mr. Stanhope, I wanted to make clear to you why…"

He held his gloved hand up in front of her face. "It is not necessary, Miss Cather. Allow me to express to you my great admiration for your fortitude. I find your resolution commendable."

She frowned. "My fortitude?"

"Yes. Your benevolent, generous conduct brought tears to my eyes. Rather than seeking the solace you required to recover from the awkward situation you found yourself in this morning, you gave up the opportunity to alleviate your anxieties in order to please your cousin. Your actions are quite exemplary. Rest well tonight. I will see you tomorrow."

Chapter Six

The next morning, John sat at the table in the breakfast room of the boarding house and took a sip of coffee. The clock chimed eight o'clock. Moments later, footsteps sounded in the entry. Mr. Pratt put his head around the door.

"Morning. Am I late?"

"Not at all. Right on time." Heavy footfalls could be heard on the stairs. "I believe Mr. Stanhope is coming now."

"Good day." He walked into the room, tugging on his neckcloth. "I had the devil of a time getting the ends to stay flat."

"Sit down, Mr. Pratt," John invited. "Would you like tea, coffee or some morsels of food? I'm certain the proprietor would allow it."

"Thank you. I ate earlier this morning, but I will have a cup of coffee."

Mr. Stanhope strode over to the front table, picking out some pieces of ham, eggs, and bites of potato, carefully arranging all the items on his plate. "Are you going to have something to eat, Mr. Rudder?"

"I had some ham and eggs earlier."

Mr. Stanhope poured himself and Mr. Pratt each a cup of coffee before sitting at the table, across from John. "What did you wish to discuss?"

John studied them for a moment before he spoke. "I

requested both of you to meet with me this morning in order to report a rather alarming circumstance. It is important for you to be aware of what occurred, Mr. Pratt, because it involves your cousin. Mr. Stanhope, it is imperative I give you the information because it relates to one of the crew."

Mr. Pratt choked on the coffee he was sipping and lowered his mug. "Ellen? What has happened?"

"You are both aware of Miss Cather's brief disappearance yesterday and the tale of the stranded kitten. That was only part of the story. After helping her out of the tree, I remembered something she had said to me when I first discovered her perched on the branch. I had a sense something had upset her, causing her to seek shelter in the woods. Upon compelling her to reveal all that occurred after she left your mother and sister, she confided the actual reason for her sudden departure from the principal walkway. Not wishing to bring additional upset to the ladies, I asked Miss Cather not to mention the other details, assuring her I would later inform both of you what occurred."

Mr. Pratt frowned. "My sense of trepidation is steadily increasing. Please continue."

John grimaced. "I fully understand your feelings of anxiety. I can assure you, other than her glove that was torn by the bark on the tree, no other harm or injury was afflicted upon your cousin. Soon after she walked away from the picnic area to check on our location, she came upon a man. I understand he was standing at the water's edge, looking out toward our boat, making disgruntled comments."

Mr. Stanhope dropped his fork onto his plate with a clatter. "Mr. Thorne?"

"Yes. Apparently, he said something demeaning about Mr. Pratt occupying a place on the boat that should have been his, as well as indicating the stroke position was to be reserved for him. Not knowing of his drunken, belligerent temperament, I believe Miss Cather thought she was consoling him when she advised Mr. Thorne it was most likely his late arrival to the boathouse that was the cause of his disappointment."

Mr. Pratt stood up. His fingers were clenched tightly into his palms. "Did he threaten her?"

"He disparaged her for speaking to him." He frowned, recalling her words. "Mr. Thorne's rough, scurrilous attitude dismayed her, and she sought shelter in the woods."

Mr. Stanhope pursed his lips before speaking. "I admonished Miss Cather for going off on her own. It appears I my words of caution were well justified."

"Let us put aside our opinions on the course of action she took and discuss Mr. Thorne," John advised, as he scowled at Mr. Stanhope. "Considering his failure to show up for practice on time yesterday after his excessive drinking at the pub on Thursday evening, and subsequent callous treatment of Miss Cather, I would like to propose we remove him from the crew and replace him with Mr. Pratt, if he is agreeable. What are your thoughts, Mr. Stanhope?"

"I am extremely displeased by Mr. Thorne's behavior. However, as I pointed out to you previously, he has much experience with rowing and was formerly a member of the Westminster School Boat Club." Mr. Stanhope furrowed his brows as he studied his half-empty plate. "I hesitate to request him to leave the crew before giving him an opportunity to redeem himself."

John turned to Mr. Pratt. "What is your inclination?"

"I can well imagine Ellen's great sense of indignation when she heard Mr. Thorne's inconsiderate remarks. Knowing her high standards for candor and decency, I am not surprised she was goaded into making the declaration." He sat down again, staring straight ahead for a moment without speaking. "After having spent a minimal amount of time in his company, I am quite certain Mr. Thorne would have made the same unguarded replies in his harsh, remorseless manner even if my mother had been present with my cousin. I am not excusing his behavior, rather acknowledging his perverse character."

"Are you saying he should be allowed to be part of our crew, even after he agitated and discomposed Miss Cather?" Mr. Stanhope questioned, with a frown.

Mr. Pratt sighed. "I worry that if Mr. Thorne is told he cannot compete in the regatta because of what he said to Ellen, he will not understand the notion of being punished for something that is a practiced standard with him. It appears a drunken state is a habitual mode for Mr. Thorne. I imagine he frequently makes similar comments to others without consideration. He could become spiteful and vindictive."

"You make a valid argument," John acknowledged. "I doubt Mr. Thorne could ever be brought to recognize anything inappropriate concerning the statements he made to Miss Cather. Should we give him another chance and not bring up the lady's involvement, Mr. Stanhope?"

"I find the notion of giving Mr. Thorne another opportunity difficult to accept." He drew a shaky breath and then released it. "However, I feel confident he will be late again today, so my current state of torment is most probably for naught."

John took a final sip of his coffee and stood up. "If you both have finished, we should make our way to the boathouse."

Mr. Stanhope spooned the last bit of egg from his plate into his mouth and then wiped his face with a serviette. "Should we prepare a missive for Mr. Thorne, declaring his expulsion from our crew, to leave with Mr. Burke if he doesn't appear?"

John glanced at the mantel clock. "I think it would be a clever stratagem to reach the boathouse a little early. We can secure our oars and have the boat ready to carry to the water at the stroke of ten o'clock. If Mr. Thorne arrives on time, it will be a pointed example to him of the serious manner in which we view our participation in the practice runs."

"Indeed." Mr. Stanhope tossed the serviette onto the table and came to his feet. "Mr. Pratt, if it becomes necessary, are you certain you wish to be part of our crew?"

"Yes, of course. I will gladly be one of your rowing team."

"Thank you! Well then, let's be off."

They arrived at the boathouse a short time later to find a crew member from another boat having an earnest discussion with Mr. Burke.

"I don't understand his attitude," the man bellowed.

"There is no justification for him to speak to you in such a mean, cantankerous manner," Mr. Burke affirmed. He studied the folded piece of parchment in his hand. "Mr. Thorne's team isn't scheduled to start for several minutes."

Mr. Stanhope stepped forward. "Did you mention Thorne? He is one of our crew."

Mr. Burke glared at him from underneath his thick, gray eyebrows. "Mr. Thorne arrived here a short time ago. He interrupted a discussion I was having with Mr. Linfield, to demand we attend to him and carry your team's boat to the dock. I informed him he needed to wait until the proper time and the rest of the crew had arrived. Then I offered a few more choice words of warning about his heavy-handed conduct."

"I apologize for Mr. Thorne's unseemly behavior." Mr. Stanhope shared an earnest look with John and Mr. Pratt. "We intend to have a serious discussion with him regarding his ill-tempered demeanor as soon as he returns."

"Mr. Thorne is not here?" Mr. Campbell strode toward them. "He quit the boarding house almost an hour ago, intending to arrive early."

John waved his hand to the others, indicating they should follow him. He strode several yards away from Mr. Burke and frowned at Mr. Campbell. "We have just learned Mr. Thorne behaved quite belligerently upon his arrival. He gave orders and demands for crew on separate crafts, as well as Mr. Burke, to carry our boat to the dock."

Mr. Campbell reached up with a shaky hand to rub his forehead. "I don't understand. He knows he must wait until all the boat's crew have arrived in order to retrieve the vessel."

"Was Mr. Thorne foxed again last night?" John studied the other man intently.

He flushed. "He had several glasses of port after dinner. Before I retired for the night, I reminded him of our start time. He promised to seek his bed immediately after finishing what remained of the wine in his glass."

"Back again to observe your cousin and his racing prowess?" a snide voice called out from behind them. "You should have stayed home. I will take my rightful place in the boat today. He will no longer be part of the crew."

John spun, to see Miss Cather standing with her aunt and cousin a few paces away. Mr. Thorne stood directly in front of the women, arms taut, pressed against the sides of his gaunt torso, fingers curled tightly into the palms of his hands.

"Sir, I must ask you to step away." Mrs. Pratt took a deep breath, holding herself straight and rigid. "You have no right to question our presence here or to address us in such a rough, uncivil manner."

Mr. Stanhope went to the group, grasped Mr. Thorne's elbow, and forced him to move back. "Have a care, sir! Ladies are present!"

"Don't tell me how to go on, you pompous ass!"

"Enough!" John strode forward, parting the two men with his hands and stepping between them. He glanced at the women, noting Miss Cather's stiff stance and stoic countenance. "Ladies, I apologize for this unseemly, discourteous display. Mr. Thorne, come to the boathouse and help us carry our vessel to the dock. We shall soon see how proficient a rower you are."

Chapter Seven

"Abigail, observe what a fine seat Mr. Rudder has!" Aunt Prudence gushed, as she stared out the window of their hired coach. "I vow I have never seen such a handsome, muscular gentleman so at ease in a saddle."

"Yes, Mother." Abigail shifted in her seat to face Ellen and rolled her eyes.

Ellen grinned at the absurd gesture while contemplating what aspect of Mr. Stanhope's form her aunt would choose to denote as admirable. She did not have long to wait.

"Ellen! I am in raptures over Mr. Stanhope's exemplary, gracious comportment." She sighed and clasped her hands together, while staring up at the roof. "I will never forget his considerate manner as he saw to your comfort and assisted you to settle in your seat before mounting his own horse."

"Indeed. He has a laudable demeanor," she commented, while privately thinking his demure, solemn behavior infuriating and often annoying. As she studied her aunt, Ellen noted the aspect of her posture. It appeared she was offering thanks to the heavens. She knew several seconds of trepidation, and her heart began to race. Taking a deep breath, Ellen deliberated over the most effective means to dissuade her aunt from persisting with her apparent, exasperating matchmaking intentions.

The carriage suddenly slowed and came to a stop. The door was thrust wide open, and Thomas appeared in the opening. He let down the steps. "Arnos Vale is a short distance away from here. We can walk there to see the field of bluebells before carrying on to the arch."

As Ellen grasped his hand and made her way out of the coach behind her aunt and cousin, she studied Thomas' sober countenance. When her cousin returned home late that morning, he had turned aside her queries about the race practice, saying he needed to change his clothes first. She decided to make another attempt to discover more information.

"Thomas…"

He put a gloved finger to his lips. "Mr. Stanhope wishes to describe the aspects of what occurred today with everyone present, before we begin our outing. Come."

They walked together, a few paces behind Aunt Prudence and Abigail, across the graveled surface toward a rustic stable. Several grooms appeared in the entranceway to lead the visitors' horses inside to a temporary shelter. Mr. Stanhope strode forward as they came to a stop in front of the building.

"Mr. Rudder will join us in a moment. He is retrieving a sketch pad from his saddle bag."

"I apologize for the delay," Mr. Rudder called out as he strolled toward them, carrying a leather-bound volume and a pencil in one hand. One of the grooms hustled past, brushing against him before turning back to apologize. "Shall we move away from this bustling corridor?"

Aunt Prudence clutched Abigail's arm, urging her forward. "Mr. Rudder, do you intend to write some verses of poetry using the bluebells as inspiration?"

He stopped walking and turned to her, grinning. "Quite a clever notion, Mrs. Pratt. I must admit, although I relish reading poems, I would never attempt to write one. I have no aptitude for combining words into a rhythmic, metered form. I merely thought to take some notes on the architectural features of the arch."

"I believe this is an ideal location for our discussion," Mr. Stanhope announced as they came to the edge of a grassy knoll. There were a few wooden benches nearby. "Ladies, would you care to sit down?"

Ellen studied Mr. Rudder with raised brows, determining to query him at the earliest opportunity concerning the precise significance of the necessity for documentation of the arch, before replying, "I am fine. Aunt, cousin?"

"No, thank you. It is not necessary, since we were seated in the carriage not long ago," Abigail answered.

"Very good. I am certain you are curious about what took place at the race practice this morning. We wished to explain the circumstances before embarking on the excursion, so as not to spoil our afternoon." Mr. Stanhope cleared his throat. "As you previously observed, Mr. Thorne arrived on time and helped us carry the boat to the water. He graciously conceded the stroke position to Mr. Rudder, taking the place in front of him. It took some time for him to match his oar strokes to our rhythm, but once he accomplished that, Mr. Thorne made a good showing during the practice."

"He didn't complain or argue with anyone?" Ellen found it hard to imagine the surly gentleman who had twice confronted her adopting a compliant manner in any situation.

"Ah! It appears Miss Cather has quickly apprehended Mr. Thorne's true character." Mr. Rudder gave her a piercing look before turning to address the others. "We returned to the dock after the practice finished, moments after another vessel arrived that had beaten us in the first race. Mr. Thorne leaped out of our boat, dropping his oars as he scrambled onto dry land. He strode up to the other crew, who were occupied with lifting their vessel out of the water, and shouted at them."

Aunt Prudence put a shaky hand up to her cheek. "Such an angry, unpleasant man!"

Ellen's meager breakfast of toast and tea tossed and churned in her stomach as she pictured the distressing scene. "What did he say?"

"It is not something fit for ladies with tender sensibilities, such as yourselves, to hear," Mr. Stanhope advised, at his most pompous.

Mr. Rudder lifted his hand, turning their attention back to him. "I will say this, with a few malicious sentences, Mr. Thorne belittled and upbraided the other crew and their performance during practice. Thankfully, there was no opportunity for him to say more. An official from the regatta committee happened to be standing nearby. Mr. Thorne was informed he would no longer be participating in the regatta and was ordered to leave the area at once."

Ellen frowned. "I imagine he immediately protested the official's decree and refused to go."

"Surprisingly, his manner changed to nothing but compliance and submission. He offered his apologies to the other crew and left with Mr. Campbell. I had waited at the boathouse for their return, and observed the entire episode," Thomas explained.

"Mr. Pratt has kindly agreed to join our crew for the duration of the practices and the regatta next Saturday." Mr. Stanhope nodded to him. "Thank you!"

"A pleasure!"

"I suggest we turn our thoughts away from rowing for the rest of the day and explore this region. Do you agree?" Mr. Rudder remarked with raised brows, as he gave an all-encompassing glance to everyone in their group.

"I believe I have spotted the field of bluebells just there under the trees." Abigail pointed toward the woods on the other side of the grassy knoll in front of them.

"Capital! Let's make our way over to the flowers." He held out his arm to her. "Perhaps you will be inspired to write a verse about them, Miss Pratt!"

Abigail blushed as she placed one gloved hand on his arm. "It is possible. However, like you, I find much more pleasure in reading the poems."

"I once thought there was nothing more thrilling than the sight of a field covered in bluebells," Aunt Prudence babbled, with a fond smile at her daughter as she strolled away with Mr. Rudder. "I have just observed something equally enchanting."

"Come, Mother." Thomas grinned at her as placed her hand on his forearm, before guiding her toward the meadow. "For now, I ask you to give all your consideration to the natural surroundings. Allow the others to make choices and manage their own futures."

Mr. Stanhope stepped up to Ellen's side, offering her his arm. "I hesitate to admonish you once again for walking about without a proper companion as you did when you first came upon Mr. Thorne, Miss Cather, but after what has transpired with him, you must see I was correct to impart my recommendations to you."

She jerked herself backward, causing him to drop his arm to his side. "You would have done better to ponder your words before you spoke, Mr. Stanhope. While I appreciate your concern for my welfare, I must remind you that only my parents, and presently my aunt in their stead, have say over what constitutes proper behavior regarding myself."

One of his bushy, red eyebrows rose and the dusting of freckles across his nose appeared to redden. "Why do you rebuke me when my sole intention is to express concern for your safety and well-being?"

She sighed. "Your apprehension pertaining to my conduct is not relevant. I am not an immature, green girl who is bent upon continually ignoring society's expectations and norms. My initial contact with Mr. Thorne was not instigated. Rather, it was by an unlucky chance that I came upon him shortly after I left my aunt's side. My comments to him were made with the intention to defuse his anxiety. I was not to know the true spiteful disposition of his character until he gave me his answer."

His somber countenance suddenly brightened, and his brown eyes twinkled. "I understand! You thought only to lessen Mr. Thorne's distress, quite a noble determination. Your worthy and gracious purpose momentarily caused you to forget the situation and your circumstances."

"You carry your presumption too far," Ellen refuted, conscious of a warm sensation on her cheeks.

"Pardon me." Mr. Rudder appeared from around one side of the knoll. "Are you both intending to join us?"

"Yes. Of course." Ellen fanned her face with one gloved hand, hoping to assuage what she imagined was an agitated, flushed countenance.

He held out his arm to her. "Come. Miss Pratt has discovered a particularly lovely grouping of bluebells. She wishes to show them to you."

"Thank you." She reached for Mr. Rudder's extended arm, grasping it like a lifeline and taking a few shaky steps forward.

"Are you ready to face the others, or would you prefer a moment of respite?" He placed his hand over hers, giving it a gentle squeeze.

Ellen paused before giving him an answer. She studied the meadow in front of them, a lush, undulating carpet of deep blue, almost purple, underpinned with green. Abigail was spinning around one especially thick clump of bluebells, the bottom of her pink walking gown just brushing the tops of the flowers. Aunt Prudence and Thomas were standing close by, smiling at her. At that moment, Mr. Stanhope strolled up to join their group, an indulgent grin suddenly curving his mouth.

"May we take the path opposite and gradually make our way around to them? I would appreciate a chance to collect myself," Ellen murmured.

"Certainly." Mr. Rudder quickly changed course. "Over the short period of our acquaintance, I have learned Mr. Stanhope can be a stickler for observing the proprieties."

"I am aware he means well, but he will soon learn I am the kind of person who chafes at others who constantly berate and admonish me."

"Incessant rebukes can be exasperating, even when one knows the words of caution are given with the best of intentions."

"I am sorry I allowed his portentous attitude to upset

me. Additionally, I tend to express myself in an awkward manner." She sighed. "I have often been accused of being austere, and I suppose my reserved demeanor comes from being an only child."

"Do you find this aspect of your personality to be a burden?"

"Yes, when an impulsive remark causes unintended pain. One such comment nearly precipitated the end of my friendship with Camille, Lady Surd."

"I find that hard to believe."

"It is true." She frowned at the ground. "I thought to impart a subtle hint to her regarding young men and their accepted frivolous activities before marriage. If not for my confession to Lord Surd and his immediate action to rectify the misunderstanding with Camille, they might never have discovered their deep love for one another."

He came to a sudden stop, turning to study her. "You were certain, beyond any reasonable doubt, that Lord Surd was participating in *frivolous activities*?"

A gentle breeze stirred the air around them and Ellen savored the subtle masculine scents of amber and musk, combined with savory notes of clove and vanilla, from Mr. Rudder's clothing. She took a moment to relish the enticing mix of fragrances as she returned his intense gaze, needing him to understand her actions. "I was not. I made a generalization after I observed him often in the company of a mature widow when we were staying in Bath last year. I informed Camille of my conviction, never, ever, thinking my words would cause her anguish."

"In what manner did you believe she would take your allusion?"

She shrugged her shoulders. "The practice is

generally acknowledged and sanctioned. I deduced my implication would not astound her or cause distress."

"Looking at the circumstances in that manner, you came to an understandable conclusion." He frowned at her. "I admit I don't remember spending much time conversing with you during our visit at Horsham House two years ago."

"There wasn't an opportunity." She chuckled. "Do you not recall? We were all outshined by Lady Sophia!"

"Ah, yes! The embodiment of conceit!" He grinned. "The lady's demeanor had altered significantly when I conversed with her at her wedding."

Ellen's mouth fell open and she put one hand against her throat. "You attended Sir Edward and Lady Sophia's wedding? Camille never mentioned you were in attendance."

"I was a witness, alongside the wife of the vicar who performed the ceremony. I am not surprised Sir Edward never spoke of the minor, trifling aspects of the wedding to his sister. It was an unforeseen, hasty event."

"Mr. Rudder! Where is your sketch book? Abigail fancies a drawing of the bluebells," Aunt Prudence called out.

"We will join you in a moment," Ellen answered. She squeezed Mr. Rudder's forearm as he guided her toward the others. "I wish to thank you for giving me the opportunity to compose myself. I am much improved."

He placed his gloved hand over her own. "A pleasure, Miss Cather. If I can ever be of assistance to you in the future, please do not hesitate to come to me. I would also advise you not to become preoccupied with worry over what you believe are sometimes your inelegant attempts to converse with others. Those who know your gracious aspect would never believe you meant to cause them anguish or pain."

"Thank you for your kind words. I will remember them always." Ellen released his arm, watching him stride away from her, across the meadow toward Abigail.

Chapter Eight

John sat down on a bench facing the arch, flipped open his sketch book, and reached for his pencil. He didn't need to capture every detail of the four statues that were set in deep niches with tentlike stone extensions perched above them. He was more interested in the shape and construction of the actual arch. Something similar would be an ideal structure, as well as an interesting focal point, to grace the far end of the lake on his property in Kent. He quickly sketched an image of the arch, adding the cursory configurations that decorated the top.

"Do you mind if I sit here while you are drawing?"

He turned to see Miss Cather standing a short distance away. "Please, make yourself comfortable. Did you not find the surrounding woods of interest? Mr. Stanhope appeared to believe they were not to be missed."

She settled herself on the opposite end of the bench and sighed. "Mr. Stanhope has determined a lady never interests herself in complex subjects such as buildings and structures or, perhaps most alarming, the study of architecture. I risked defacing his notions of respectability and openly disagreed with this perception. He became quite disgruntled at my unalterable stance and recommended I join you."

He put his sketch book and pencil down. "I recall,

you were quite enthusiastic about a book you read on the architecture of Bath. Is this a recent preoccupation?"

She frowned while gazing straight ahead. "I have always enjoyed perusing books describing unique structures. I suppose I became enthralled with the subject while we were visiting Horsham House. One morning before the daily activities began, Sir Edward and I discussed the history of his home. He mentioned his father's interest in builders' pattern books and Greek antiquities to me. I imagine my overly enthusiastic reaction to this news caused him to graciously allow me unlimited access to his library and his late father's collection during the remainder of our stay there."

"I am sorry I wasn't cognizant of that conversation. I too would have enjoyed looking over those volumes."

She turned to face him, pointing to his book. "You surprised me when you walked out of the stables with this. The sketch of the bluebells you made for Abigail was quite impressive. Now I discover you here creating detailed drawings of the arch. I had no idea you had a serious interest in illustration or structures."

"I grew up on my family's estate near Reading. For two years, just before I left to attend Harrow, my parents procured a tutor for me who also happened to be an accomplished artist. Mr. Ware and I spent many afternoons, after I had finished my studies for the day, drawing our impressions of surrounding landscapes. That is where my attraction to sketching began. I must admit, my engrossment in construction is quite recent. Last year, my father gifted me a fifteen-acre property in Kent, just outside of Rochester. It was left to him by my grandfather and once held a hunting lodge, but that structure burned down twenty years ago, not long after

Granddad passed away. Several tenant homes and stables are all that is presently on the property, used by the employees and their families who tend the fields and take care of the horses."

"A generous bequest! I don't recall, are you also an only child?"

"No. My older brother lives on the family estate. Charles is married with two children. He keeps busy with the management of that property and takes occasional trips to London, where my parents reside most of the year." He chuckled. "The provision of land of my own came at an opportune time. I had become thoroughly jaded with my aimless existence in the metropolis."

She gaped at him. "You astonish me! I understand you have a wide circle of friends. You and Lord Surd are quite close. I imagined you to be continually occupied with engagements and attending a variety of parties and balls in London. Additionally, you make time to perform favors for acquaintances, such as being a witness at Sir Edward's and Lady Sophia's wedding."

He grinned at her. "You are describing the issue most accurately. At the risk of sounding snobbish, I came to realize I tended to live my life for others' pleasure, rarely for my own. I made certain to attend all the events I was invited to, even if it meant going to more than one party in an evening, often arriving at my lodgings at dawn, exhausted. I often dined in the clubs with my friends, almost never spending a relaxing night on my own at home. I frequently joined acquaintances in galivanting to various events outside the city. My mother was instrumental in planning my participation at the Horsham House gathering. She asked me to be present as a favor to her friend Lady Collins, Lady Surd's mother. I agreed several days ago to be one of the crew for this regatta when the fourth member of Mr. Stanhope's team suddenly injured his arm in a carriage accident. Luckily, my father is quite perceptive. He sensed my need to find a purpose in life and presented me with the deed to the property. I intend to hire builders and start the process of development there this summer."

"Oh, lovely! Quite a providential opportunity for you!" She smiled at him as she clasped her gloved hands together in her lap. "Do you have any sense of the style you desire? Do you prefer Neoclassical or Neo-Gothic? Or perhaps the austere Palladian manner? You must be certain to use sash windows!"

He stared at her. "Miss Cather, I am impressed! You are extremely well-versed in the various styles of architecture."

"Make certain you never repeat that opinion in Mr. Stanhope's hearing." She chuckled and then pointed to his sketch pad. "You have drawn a good representation of the undersized, shallow ornamentations at the top of the arch. Do you intend to embellish the roofline of your home with something similar?"

He frowned as he stared down at the piece of vellum. "I confess I haven't come to a decision on the style or size of the main structure. There is a lake on one edge of the property. I thought to construct a folly on the far shore, facing east, where one could sit on a warm summer's afternoon and contemplate a pleasing view of the house. I visualize the house perched above the water, partially framed at the back by a grove of ancient elm trees."

"Your image sounds delightful."

"Tell me, why do you recommend sash windows?"

She leaned forward, her light blue eyes suddenly warming like a cloudless sky in the middle of summer. "They are imperative for controlling ventilation throughout the rooms, considering the variable climate of the four seasons. The proportions are also better suited if you should decide on a classical style of facade for your home."

"I have a concept in my mind of a three-story brick structure with twelve-paned windows and two Ionic columns framing the front door with a fanlight above. Is that considered classical?"

"Greek classical architecture was constructed with the fundamentals of order and symmetry in mind. For your home to be considered classical, the brick would need to be covered in stucco or painted plaster, to resemble marble. In that way, the surface becomes more symmetrical and balanced."

"Hmm." He wrinkled his brow as he deliberated over what she had said. "I am intrigued by the different choices and styles. I know you have visited Bath. What manner would you classify those structures in the city that are built of Bath stone?"

"Ah, yes! The buildings in Bath are quite lovely, and graced by such a warm, honey colored stone! The most common architectural technique used there is known as the Palladian style. Also valued for its symmetry, direct perspectives, and formal, classical style, the Palladian is named after the Venetian architect Andrea Palladio."

"I imagine if I used Bath stone on the facade of my home, it would not be covered with stucco or paint?"

"No, never! Bath stone should always be left in its natural state. It is far too beautiful to be shrouded with another material. However, I would urge you to consider the cost of transporting the stone from Bath quarries to your property in Kent. I imagine it would substantially increase the overall sum for building your structure."

"You point out many interesting options and offer some valid issues to consider before I build. Is there anything else you would recommend me to be cognizant regarding the design or formation?"

"Do you plan to marry and have a family? If so, I would suggest adding another story to the main house, for a nursery." She blushed. "I'm sorry. I must apologize for my presumption. I did warn you about my awkward attempts at conversation."

He chuckled. "There is nothing for you to regret. I certainly intend to have a wife and children in the future. Additionally…"

"What is wrong?"

He frowned. "I had forgotten. A country house needs to provide lodging for the servants."

"Certainly. Unless a servant happens to be from one of the families who live in the tenant houses on the property, a place to wash, sleep, and store their uniforms and other clothing would be required."

"I had planned on a housekeeper's quarters in the basement. I must remember to include a butler's pantry, as well as a servants' hall. I suppose the chambermaids would sleep in rooms in the attics above the nursery?"

"Miss Cather, Mr. Rudder!" Mr. Stanhope appeared from behind the arch and strode toward them. "I have arranged for tea to be served in a private parlor at the Black Castle. No doubt you are parched and weary after spending so long in aimless discussion about this edifice, Miss Cather. I apologize for not arriving sooner to escort you inside."

"I don't intend…" She slowly came to her feet. "As you wish, Mr. Stanhope. I have thoroughly enjoyed our discussion, Mr. Rudder. Do you join us?"

"A pleasure. Yes, momentarily. I need to add a few details to my sketch." John stood up from the bench, bending over to peer through the arch at the Black Castle just beyond. "The front of the castle is quite unique. Do you happen to know the material that was used, Miss Cather?"

She paused in the act of putting her hand on Mr. Stanhope's arm to turn to smile at him. "I do, Mr. Rudder. The bricks are made from slag waste from a nearby factory owned by William Reeve. He smelted brass and copper."

"Oh, goodness!" Mr. Stanhope shuddered and closed his eyes for a moment, before opening them once more and firmly placing Miss Cather's gloved hand on his arm. "Come! It is past time for you to have your tea!"

Chapter Nine

Ellen sat forward on the edge of her chair in the sitting room to look out the window and study the fluffy, white clouds skimming across the sky on Monday afternoon. It was certainly breezy outside, but no storm clouds appeared on the horizon portending rain. Sunday had been spent quietly with no visitors. After they returned from church, Ellen's thoughts were preoccupied with the discussion she and Mr. Rudder had the day before, about his plans for his property. He seemed unsure about the design of the house as well as the configuration of the floorplans. She was eager to advise him further on the various options she thought wise to consider, but she hesitated to approach him, believing she would appear too bold or self-assertive.

A notion had formed in her mind this morning during breakfast, as her cousin and aunt had been engrossed with a discussion about the upcoming dance at the assembly rooms tomorrow night. While they were distracted with the crucial decision of which of Abigail's gowns was most flattering to her fair complexion, Ellen determined it would be quite useful to obtain a builder's pattern book from the circulating library, one which showed preferential floorplans for country houses. She could present it to Mr. Rudder as a useful tool in his research. The one problem was how to walk to the library and procure such an item without Aunt Prudence's knowledge. On her previous visits accompanied by that lady, Ellen had pointedly avoided the section containing volumes on architecture. She had already brought plenty of censure down upon her head for taking an inordinate interest in structures and could imagine her aunt's displeasure and vexation if she were to bring a book home on the subject.

A splendid opportunity had suddenly come to pass for her to leave the house. After requesting her maid to assist her to wash and dry her hair, Abigail went to her room. Shortly afterward, Aunt Prudence announced her intention to take a nap.

Ellen tapped one finger against the arm of the chair in frustration. She could not go to the library by herself. Should she ask Cook's daughter, who worked in the house as a chambermaid, to accompany her?

"Cousin! Well met! Have you had a busy day today?" Thomas grinned at her as he strolled into the room.

"Thomas! You have finished practice? Please, will you escort me to the library?" She surged to her feet.

"We easily won all three of the races, thank you for inquiring, Ellen," he answered wryly. "Why such haste? Surely Abigail and Mother will accompany you there?"

She reached out to grip his arm. "It is important that I obtain a certain book. Your mother and sister are otherwise occupied. I promise to be quick."

He sighed. "Very well. Let us be on our way before I regret my decision to squire you."

"Thank you! One moment..." Ellen picked up her skirts to stride out of room and up the stairs to retrieve her reticule and pelisse from her bedchamber. She rejoined Thomas in the entry a few minutes later.

"Shall we be off?" He offered her his arm.

Griggs opened the door for them.

They quickly made their way around Queen's Square and down to King Street toward the center of town.

As they walked, Ellen recalled Thomas's earlier comment regarding the race practice. "Your time on the water today was certainly successful. Is there a reason why you and the rest of the crew performed so well?"

He grinned at her. "Other than my presence on the boat? I believe we all felt a measure of solace knowing Mr. Thorne would not be making an appearance today. His unsettling, coarse mannerisms cast a pall over what should otherwise be a convivial exercise. Those circumstances changed this morning. We were able to work together with smooth, flawless unity and win."

"Has Mr. Thorne quit town?"

He frowned. "Mr. Campbell could not say. He has not encountered him since Mr. Thorne was ordered to leave the dock yesterday."

"I will be quite relieved to know he has gone." She stopped in front of the library entrance. A group of several young ladies appeared in the doorway, followed by an elderly matron. The girls were chattering together, each clutching a book. Ellen waited until they had passed by before turning back to her cousin. "Are you coming inside?"

Thomas was studying the group of women as they strolled away down the street. "No. I will wait here."

Smiling as she observed one of the ladies pivot to give Thomas a coy glance before turning back to her companions, Ellen picked up the edges of her skirts and marched up the steps to the library.

Striding to the shelves holding books on architecture, Ellen promptly found the section containing volumes on structures and construction methods. Within this cluster of books, she spotted two on floorplans. One was titled, *Optimal Use of Space for a Gentlemen's Townhome* and the other read, *Country House Floorplans*. She decided the volume relating to a country house was much more appropriate to Mr. Rudder's needs. Without further consideration, Ellen took the book off the shelf and made her way to the counter. She stopped in the middle of the aisle when her gaze caught the title of another book—*Frankenstein*. With a sigh, she picked it up. She had told Mr. Stanhope she would read the story. It would be vastly impertinent to disregard her stated intention.

The clerk raised his bushy eyebrows when he noted her selections, but he didn't make a comment. After writing the information on her subscription card, he handed the volumes back to her.

"Thank you. Good day." She made her way out the door and down the front steps. Thomas stood where she had left him.

"You were certainly quick."

"I knew exactly what I required." She clutched the volumes to her chest so he wouldn't see the book on floorplans and ask probing questions. "Shall we make our way back?"

He offered her his arm. "Let's take the walkway that passes in front of the tavern. It is a shorter distance."

They strolled along the street without speaking. They were nearing the tavern as Ellen deliberated how best to hand over the book to Mr. Rudder.

"I will not return to London before the regatta is

over. I must be on that boat! My father intends to be a spectator on Saturday. He is inordinately proud of my rowing prowess!" The snide comment was followed by an ear-piercing guffaw.

Thomas came to a sudden stop. He clutched Ellen's arm, and quickly turned around, striding back down the street several paces, pulling her with him.

"Was that...?"

He grimaced and nodded his head. "Mr. Thorne? Yes. I need to inform the others of his intention. I will escort you home first."

"No! I must go with you."

"You cannot accompany me to a gentlemen's lodging house, Ellen."

"I will not go inside. We can let them know what was said on the front steps of the establishment. Hurry! We are wasting time standing here arguing."

Thomas glared at her, his lips pressed together, before exhaling loudly. "Come along."

Ellen did her best to keep up with Thomas' long strides, following him back to King Street and then down a few blocks to Colston Avenue. Once there, he turned to his right, passing several buildings. He came to a stop in front of a three-story brick structure. Facing the quay, it had a wide deck containing several caned chairs and a couple of rustic tables.

"Take a seat. I will ascertain if Mr. Stanhope and Mr. Rudder are on the premises and ask them to step outside." Thomas opened the front door, firmly shutting it behind him.

Ellen sat down on one of the chairs at the rear of the porch, keeping the books tucked face down on her lap, underneath her reticule. She contemplated several boats as they made their way down the quay, until the sounds of footsteps and male voices could be heard coming from inside the lodging house. The door opened and all three men emerged. Mr. Stanhope led the group, outfitted in informal sailor attire: a navy-blue, single-breasted coat over a high-collared linen shirt, a knotted yellow neckcloth tied at his throat, loose-fitting gray trousers, and his round-toed leather shoes with oval buckles.

"Miss Cather! I am astounded Mr. Pratt permitted you to accompany him here! I am quite discomposed by the notion." Mr. Stanhope put a shaking hand in his coat pocket and brought out his handkerchief, wiping it across his forehead.

"I am afraid I left my cousin with no choice in the matter." She frowned at him. "I find your reaction to my current situation, reclining in a chair on a porch, outside in accessible, public surroundings, quite absurd."

Mr. Rudder stepped in front of Mr. Stanhope. "I understand you and Mr. Pratt have something of import to relay to us."

Ellen glanced appreciatively at Mr. Rudder. He had found an opportunity to change his attire. A pristine white muslin shirt, topped by a loosely tied cravat, accentuated the strong, smooth column of his throat. A chocolate-brown tailcoat with tight sleeves highlighted his robust arms. A matching waistcoat covered his broad chest. Tan breeches tucked into shiny black Hessian boots drew attention to his firm, muscular thighs. She took a deep breath to steady a sudden sense of breathlessness before answering, "Yes. Yes, we do. We heard Mr. Thorne make some disquieting comments."

His eyebrows shot up and his stance became rigid. "Did he threaten you?"

"Thankfully, he was not aware of our presence," Thomas replied as he made his way around one of the chairs to lean against the front railing. "Ellen and I were returning home from an errand in town and we passed by The Lamb and Anchor. Mr. Thorne was inside, his thundering, sneering tone of voice easily recognizable. He stated he would not be returning to London until the regatta was over. He also said he intends to be part of the crew. Apparently, his father is coming on Saturday to watch him participate in the race."

Mr. Rudder frowned. "Do you know who Mr. Thorne was speaking to?"

Thomas shook his head. "I made no attempt to discover. I thought it prudent to leave the area as quickly as possible, bearing in mind Ellen's presence. I assume it was Mr. Campbell."

Mr. Stanhope began to pace back and forth on the deck while tugging at the ends of his neckcloth. "We must report this transgression immediately to the regatta committee. Mr. Thorne was banned from participating in the race."

It was obvious Mr. Stanhope had forgotten, for the moment, his concern over what Ellen guessed he imagined were her maidenly sentiments. She took the opportunity to speak. "Do you think it possible that Mr. Thorne would dare to appear at the boathouse after the warning given to him by the race official? Surely the man in charge of the vessels would send him away?"

Thomas reached out to grip the back of one of the chairs. "Ellen, you heard what he said in the tavern and are familiar with his abundant, unpleasant personality traits. Do you think a simple verbal warning, even from a person of authority, would keep Mr. Thorne from getting the outcome he believes he deserves?"

Mr. Rudder crossed his arms across his chest and walked across the porch to face the water. He didn't speak for several seconds. "You make an excellent point, Mr. Pratt. It is certainly an impossible task to reason with someone of Mr. Thorne's drunken, resentful aspect. We observed the optimal results today when we raced with no interference from him. Should we continue as our crew performed this morning, without deliberations and worry over Mr. Thorne, striving for the best possible outcome at the end of each day's practice?"

Mr. Stanhope put a hand to his forehead. "Are you recommending we take no action to thwart his imprudent threats?"

"Yes. We will make a move only if Mr. Thorne should try to force his way onto the boat. Until then, all our attention and effort should be on completing the best possible race."

"I agree. It is a waste of time for us to contemplate Mr. Thorne's many troubles and quandaries and how he might reciprocate." Thomas strolled over to Mr. Stanhope. "I noticed you have a way of holding your forearms up, parallel with the oars that gives you more control. Could you explain your method to me?"

The two men quickly became engrossed in the discussion. Taking advantage of the ideal opportunity, Ellen stood up from her chair and strode over to Mr. Rudder, holding the book on floorplans out in front of her. "I hope you don't think me presumptuous, but I wanted to give this to you. I believe if you peruse the examples of floorplans, it will assist you to determine the best choice for your own needs."

With raised brows, he took hold of the volume and

studied it. "Thank you, Miss Cather! I appreciate your thoughtfulness. Is this from your own collection?"

"A pleasure." She hastily looked around to check if the others were still talking. Reassured, she turned back. "No, no. It is from the circulating library. When you have finished with the book, I would be grateful if you would wrap it in paper before returning it to me. My aunt would be most displeased if she discovered I ignored her directive against concerning myself with construction and architecture."

He chuckled while tucking the volume under one arm. "You obtained this book for me knowing you risked Mrs. Pratt's censure? Admirable! There is certainly just cause to be inordinately grateful to you."

Chapter Ten

John studied himself in the mirror. He hoped he
would pass any cursory scrutiny from other attendees at
the dance. In case he should be invited to such an event,
he had packed a dark gray, double-breasted cutaway
coat. Mrs. Dowding had graciously agreed to starch and
iron his white muslin shirt. Black pantaloons covered his
legs, with matching stockings and soft black leather
pumps on his feet. Perhaps his cravat was tied in a
manner that lacked the exceptional flair his valet's
superior skills could provide. However, a small assembly
in Bristol would not command the same intense scrutiny
of one's attire as often occurred at a London ball. It was
doubtful anyone would notice.

John picked up his hat and quit the room, closing the
door securely behind him. He mulled over today's
practice as he made his way down the stairs. The races
had proved to be just as productive as Monday's had
been. Their boat had come in first in all three
competitions.

"You turned yourself out quite fine."

He bowed to Mr. Stanhope, who was waiting for
him in the entry, rising to consider his friend's azure-blue
wool frock coat worn over a silver waistcoat and frilled
shirt, tied with a stock at his throat. His stout legs were
covered by buff knee-breeches, white stockings, and
black pumps adorned with square, silver buckles. He

held his gloves and top hat in one hand. "You as well."

"Mr. Pratt gave me directions to the assembly rooms. The others are hiring a carriage and will meet us. Shall we make our way there?" Mr. Stanhope stepped to the front door and pulled it open.

John followed him outside, pausing on the deck to pull on his gloves and place his hat on his head. "Are the rooms close to the water?"

"No. They are located on the hill behind us, in a suburb just outside Bristol known as Clifton. We take Queens Road to Richmond Hill, then over to Merchants Road. The rooms are on the Mall, a short distance from there."

"Before I arrived here, I never pictured Bristol with prominent inclines," John commented as they strolled up Queens Road. "Somehow I believed that type of landscape was confined to the Lake District."

"There aren't many places in Great Britain with extrusive features," Mr. Stanhope observed, as he turned up Richmond Hill and then led the way over to Merchants Road. "It is not surprising you never imagined the city in that way." He nodded toward a building across the street. "I believe the place we are looking for is over there."

John studied the structure from their vantage point. Covered with ashlar limestone in the classical style, there were two stories and a basement. He noted, with great interest, the six giant Ionic columns and the five twelve-paned upper windows between them, with extremely ornate windows below on the principal floor. The outer and central windows had pediments with foliate consoles above them, while the second and fourth ones had canted bays, Ionic pilaster jambs and entablature. The windows on the basement level were semicircular, arched. The central doorway had coved reveals and wrought-iron grilles.

"Good evening. Mother sent me outside to make certain you had not lost your way," Mr. Pratt called to them as he stood in his black coat and dark brown breeches in front of the entrance.

"That is quite considerate of her," Mr. Stanhope replied as they walked across the street toward him. "As you can see, we had no problem finding the location."

"I trust we are not late?" John inquired as they stepped inside the entry.

"Not at all. The first set is just about to finish." Tom strolled into the assembly room.

As he entered the chamber behind Mr. Pratt, John noted the two fireplaces at opposite ends of the space, each with a variegated marble surround. The sides of the surrounds were curved in the Empire style. The mantels were also marble and of a solid dark green hue. A high, arched ceiling surged above him; two large, gleaming chandeliers dangled overhead. Twelve classical columns, at least fifteen feet in height, covered with a mixture of olive green and a pale pink to resemble marble, graced the space against the walls at precise intervals throughout the room. Their intricate capitals were painted gold.

The music came to a stop, the couples bowed and curtsied to one another, and the dance floor quickly emptied.

"Miss Cather! You look quite beautiful," Mr. Stanhope gushed. He bowed to her as she walked toward them after thanking her dance partner. "Dare I hope you have the next set free?"

John bowed as well and then studied her attire with lowered eyelids. Miss Cather's charming, graceful proportions were adorned in a white silk gown trimmed at the bottom with three bands of white lace, intermittently adorned with small bouquets of pink silk roses. Her thick blonde hair was swept high onto the crown of her head, encircled by a garland of white roses. A profusion of curls enticingly brushed the sides of her smooth cheeks. A string of pearls wrapped around her neck, dangling just above the low bodice.

"Gladly!" She smiled at Mr. Stanhope and placed her gloved hand on his arm.

"Mother and Abigail are sitting on the other side of the room."

Mr. Pratt's voice jerked John out of his reverie. Miss Cather's dazzling aspect had stunned him. He cleared his throat. "Oh. Yes, of course. Please lead the way."

John followed Mr. Pratt around the perimeter of the room. They paused occasionally to allow his companion to introduce him to notable acquaintances who resided in the city. He greeted them in a perfunctory manner, all the while admonishing himself to return his complete attention to the present.

"Here we are."

"Mr. Rudder! How elegant you look!" Mrs. Pratt exclaimed. She hastily rose to stand in front of her chair, causing the profusion of white ostrich feathers adorning the turban on her head to bob up and down. "Here is Abigail."

"Mrs. Pratt, Miss Pratt." He bowed to both ladies, noting Mrs. Pratt's puce-colored headgear provided a startling contrast to the white plumes. She turned away when an elderly matron approached and engaged her in conversation.

"Good evening, Mr. Rudder." Miss Pratt smiled up at him from her seat next to her mother.

"May I have the next dance, Miss Pratt?" He contemplated her evening gown of white crepe, finished at the bottom with a band of tiny yellow daisies and green leaves. Her black hair was plaited high on the crown of her head, the interwoven strands secured with a broad emerald- green satin ribbon. "You look lovely."

"Thank you, Mr. Rudder. Yes, I am free for the next set."

He took the chair next to her. "Have you had an opportunity to read any of Coleridge's poetry?"

She studied her gloved hands as they rested in her lap with pursed lips. "Yes, I have. When I read his works, I confess I do not experience the elation and satisfaction I feel as I peruse Mr. Wordsworth's. I sense a sadness or despair in his tone."

"I agree with your sentiments. It is my understanding Coleridge suffers from a dependency upon laudanum, which causes him to endure a grievous depression of spirit."

"That would explain the perception of melancholy and wretchedness his poetry conjures in my mind." She sighed. "It is no wonder I prefer the feelings of joy and contentment I experience when reading Wordsworth's works."

"I find myself wishing to study a bit of poetry when I hear your descriptions, Miss Pratt, which is surprising since I rarely delve into that style of written matter," Mr. Stanhope remarked, who suddenly appeared in front of them with Miss Cather at his side.

"The set is finished," Miss Cather clarified.

"Then I believe it is our turn to dance." John stood, offering his arm to Miss Pratt.

They took their places in the center of the floor and were soon joined by several other couples, including Miss Cather and Mr. Pratt. The band began to play the first jaunty notes, and the couples joined hands, circling each other in the first steps of the cotillion dance.

There was little opportunity to converse. Adjacent partners were exchanged, gloved hands were caught behind each other's backs while twirling to return once more to the original circle, before grasping the beginning partner's hand and dancing across to the other side and again forming the circle.

John observed Miss Cather as she faultlessly performed the steps. The two of them had danced together at the party Lady Collins improvised at Horsham House, but he had never been at a formal ball or assembly with her in attendance. Their gazes suddenly locked across the dance floor and she smiled at him, her blue eyes gleaming with an unexpected warmth.

After several more turns across the floor, the dance came to an end. The gentlemen bowed and the ladies curtsied to their partners.

"Oh!" Miss Pratt exclaimed as they walked toward the chairs. She came to an abrupt halt, lifting her right foot up off the floor. "I believe I have a pebble inside my slipper."

"A moment." Mr. Pratt moved forward. "If Mr. Rudder will escort Miss Cather, I will help you over to the seat next to Mother."

"Of course." John relinquished Miss Pratt to her brother's care and then held out his arm to Miss Cather. "Shall we take a turn about the room while the others see to resolving your cousin's momentary discomfort?"

"I would appreciate a chance to stroll. Thank you." She placed her hand on his arm. "Did you have an opportunity to take note of the interesting facade of this building when you arrived?"

"Yes, indeed. I made note of the alternating ornamentations between the outer, central and second and fourth windows. Is that unusual?"

"It certainly does not follow the norm or the definition of classical symmetry. It was designed and built by Francis Howard Greenway, who was transported to Australia in 1814 as a convict for the crime of forgery."

John raised his brows as he heard the surprising details. "Forgery? Do you know the circumstances of his arrest?"

"The details are cursory. I understand he became bankrupt in 1809 and was advised by 'friends' to plead guilty to forging a financial document in 1812."

"Unfortunate. He obviously had great aptitude as an architect."

"I agree. Do not despair." She smiled at him before continuing, "I recently read an account of his activities since arriving in New South Wales. I learned that, between 1816 and 1818, he designed and built the Macquarie Lighthouse on the South Head near the entrance to Port Jackson."

"I am quite happy to know Mr. Greenway has been able to continue working on other projects."

John led Miss Cather over to rejoin their group. Miss Pratt appeared restored and comfortable once more. He noticed Mr. Stanhope sat in the chair next to her. They were deep in conversation. Mrs. Pratt observed them with a fond smile on her face. Mr. Pratt stood nearby watching the dancers.

"Isn't that Mr. Campbell?" Miss Cather asked, before releasing his arm and taking a seat. "He appears to be gesturing to us."

Mr. Stanhope came to his feet. "Mr. Campbell? Where?"

"I see him," Mr. Pratt replied. "He is standing near the entry. Shall I go and discover what he requires?"

John frowned. "I think it would be wise for the three of us to go speak to him. I imagine he has some information about the races tomorrow. Ladies, please excuse us. We will return momentarily."

"May I accompany you?" Miss Cather stood up once more and gripped his forearm while staring intently into his eyes.

"If you insist." He was no match for the warm, pleading expression reflected in her blue eyes.

They made their way to the front entry where Mr. Campbell stood waiting.

"Good evening." John noticed his gloved hands were tugging nervously at the edges of his coat. "Let us step outside."

He and Miss Cather lead the way while the other men followed behind them.

After securely closing the front door, Mr. Stanhope spoke out, "What has happened?"

"It…" Mr. Campbell paused. "I hesitate to speak of the circumstance in front of the lady."

Miss Cather cleared her throat. "If the matter involves Mr. Thorne, I wish to be apprised of any unseemly incidents he played a part in. Withholding the information would cause me terrible distress."

Mr. Campbell nodded. "It is Mr. Thorne. He quit the lodging house immediately after dinner without finishing his customary bottle of brandy. I thought it extremely odd and decided to follow him."

"I commend your prudent sentiments," Mr. Stanhope remarked. "Where did he go?"

"To Hotwells Dockyard on the other side of the floating harbor, just down the hill from here." Mr. Campbell put a shaky hand up to his neckcloth. "I understand contemptuous, disdainful sailors who can't find work often gather there."

"It is certainly not a safe part of town," Mr. Pratt acknowledged, with a grimace.

"I observed Mr. Thorne approach a massive, burly man. Even from where I watched from several feet away, I could see his arms were thick and broad, like tree trunks." Mr. Campbell paused and took a deep breath. "Their voices were muffled at first, but I managed to move closer without being seen. I heard Mr. Thorne say, '*The man accompanied his mother, sister, and cousin to the assembly rooms in a hired carriage. He will return to the stables shortly to request the carriage for their return home. You are to waylay him and pummel him. Be certain to break at least one of his arms.*' There was further discussion I couldn't hear, and then Mr. Thorne threw a coin on the ground and walked away."

At that moment, a large human shape suddenly emerged from the bushes that edged the opposite side of the road. The moon rising from behind, cast an eerie shadow onto the enormous silhouette.

John placed his free hand on Miss Cather's and whispered, "There he is."

The man sauntered out into the middle of the street

and stared at them. He had curly brown hair framing a singularly grisly countenance, his forehead high and thick over bushy brows perched above dark, deep-set eyes. A large, bulging nose, with a misshapen wart dangling from its end, dominated his face. His mouth, surrounded by thickset lips, was closed tightly in a forbidding expression. His hair draped down upon his shoulders in a tangled jumble underneath a tall, wide-brimmed hat. A frayed neckcloth drooped from his burly throat and hung over his tattered waistcoat. His broad chest and massive, muscular arms were barely restrained inside a blue sailor's jacket, decorated with brass buttons and closed mariner's cuffs. Thick, sturdy legs were encased in trousers meant to be worn loosely but, on this man, stretched taut. His gigantic feet were partially covered with what once had been sturdy black leather shoes. The material had split away from the sole, exposing several enormous toes. He carried a formidable cudgel in his right hand.

"One of you must be the gent I was asked ter trounce. I wasn't expectin' no crowd."

John cleared his throat as he eyed the rustic weapon the man gripped in his brawny fingers. Miss Cather's hand clutched his arm. "There is a lady present. None of us wishes to fight you."

"There ain't goin' to be no brawl. I'm not one ter harm someone who hasn't tried ter injure me first. That drunken bloke saw only what he assumed I was when he looked at me. He thought nothin' of telling me to lay my fists on someone else. Certain sure, I'm a big man. I've always been this way. My father once told me I was too heavy for him to carry a few months after I was born!"

"He will be severely reprimanded for what he tried

to have done," Mr. Stanhope vowed.

The man snorted. "That's none of my concern. I want you ter remind that nasty bloke, once he learns he didn't get his way an' then starts whinin' about payin' good money for someone to do a job and getting cheated on, that I told him I didn't want ter 'ave any part of it. But he wouldn't listen. He told me what he wanted done and then left after throwin' his money on the ground at my feet. Here's his guinea. Give it back ter him with my compliments."

"A moment, sir," Mr. Stanhope called out. "The race officials should be advised of this matter. What do you advise, Mr. Rudder?"

John studied the man as he stood in the street, holding the coin outward, clutched between two beefy fingers. "Mr…?"

"I go by Slade. Oliver Slade."

"Mr. Slade. The person who approached you will be punished. We need to record what you have told us on paper and submit the account to persons of authority. If Mr. Campbell were to write down all that you and he witnessed tonight, would you sign the paper to indicate your agreement to the statements?"

He gnashed his burly lips together before answering, "I can write my name. You're certain there won't be no blame attached ter me?"

"None at all," John assured him. "This man has previously been banned by the officials. News of his latest stunt will come as no surprise, unfortunately."

He didn't answer for several seconds. "I agree ter yer proposition."

"Excellent! With your assistance, we should be able to have him removed from the city." John turned to Mr.

Campbell. "Are you familiar with the Mardyke? I understand it is a tavern a short walk from Cumberland Basin. I heard Mr. Burke say he and a few of the officials meet there in the evenings for a pint."

"I knows where it is. I lives in a room upstairs," Mr. Slade spoke out.

"Very good! Mr. Campbell, accompany Mr. Slade there, locate paper, pen, and ink, and record the circumstances that you both were witness to. Once you have written down each rendering, you both must sign it. If the officials are there, give it to them. If not, bring the paper to racing practice tomorrow morning."

"Who is to be takin' this here coin from me?"

"I appreciate your honesty and refusal to participate in this evil plot, Mr. Slade. I will ensure the guinea gets back to Mr. Thorne." Mr. Stanhope plucked the coin from the man's massive palm and dropped it in his waistcoat pocket.

"Mr. Pratt, you and I will go order the carriage. Mr. Stanhope, please escort Miss Cather inside. Mrs. Pratt is most likely becoming anxious." John placed Ellen's hand on the other man's arm, being careful to avoid her gaze. As much as he might wish for her enduring company, it was past time to relinquish her to another.

Chapter Eleven

Ellen contemplated her image in the mirror as her cousin's maid finished securing her hair in a large comb on the crown of her head and stepped back. "Thank you, Fanny. You have done well. Please go attend your mistress."

The gentlemen had agreed to meet them at the theater on King Street tonight. She looked upon the occasion with trepidation. It was past time to face what, if any, were her feelings for Mr. Stanhope and Mr. Rudder. When she arrived in Bristol almost a fortnight ago, marriage had been a subject far from the forefront of her thoughts. Time had passed, the years advancing without the prospect of having a husband and a family of her own being given much notice. Her parents never placed any pressure on her to find a gentleman to marry. Her father's brother's oldest son was safely installed as his heir and would inherit the family estate in Richmond.

She sighed. Despite her discomfort with Aunt Prudence's tactics, at her advanced age of twenty, Ellen now recognized she would soon be considered *on the shelf.* A few years on, she would be described as a *spinster* and relegated to spending the rest of her days living with her parents. When they were gone, she would be sent to live in an arbitrary relative's household, occupying her days with darning torn sheets and repairing worn stockings. She must marry to avoid such an unpalatable fate.

She stood and shook out the skirts of her white satin evening gown, reaching for her gloves, reticule, and shawl that Fanny had placed on a nearby chair. It was time to join the others downstairs in the dining room. Her aunt had deemed it advisable to have a light repast before heading out to the theater.

Ellen made her way down the stairs and along the passageway to the dining room. The butler was before her to open the door. She handed him the loose articles, to be collected upon their departure. "Thank you, Griggs."

She walked into the room, to discover her aunt sitting by herself. "Am I early, Aunt?"

"No, no! Take a seat. I imagine Abigail will be here shortly. Thomas has gone to the Rummer to have a pint of ale with the gentlemen and discuss strategy for tomorrow's practice. He will be here presently to escort us to the theater."

Ellen sat in her usual chair. "I look forward to the occasion."

The door opened and Abigail walked into the room. Her soft peach-colored crepe round gown swirled across the tops of her white kid leather slippers, causing the broad trimming of white satin in a scroll pattern at the bottom of the skirt to resemble waves lapping against the shoreline. Her hair was done in a coronet style secured by a thick braid at the front. "I am sorry I took so long."

"You both look lovely." Aunt Prudence paused as a serving maid came into the room carrying a platter of sliced beef, boiled potatoes, and carrots, as well as a pot of tea and three cups. The maid placed everything on the table, curtsied, and left. Aunt poured tea into their cups.

"Come, have something to eat."

Abigail took her place at the table. "What play are we seeing tonight, Mother?"

"*Mary Stuart*. It depicts the last days of Mary, Queen of Scots. I understand the lead is to be played by Miss Desmond. I thought her quite excellent as Desdemona in *Othello*."

Ellen spooned some of the vegetables and a slice of beef onto her plate. "I enjoyed seeing *King Lear* at the theater last year."

Abigail's fork hovered over a piece of carrot as she stared blankly at the wall in front of her. "Oh, yes! Edmund Kean was divine. He acts with such intense emotion."

Aunt Prudence wiped her mouth with a serviette and cleared her throat. "Before Thomas returns, I wish to discuss something of relevance with you both. It concerns Mr. Rudder and Mr. Stanhope. I have observed both gentlemen, their interactions with each of you and managed to glean some information about their families as well. I have not altered my previous surmise and believe Mr. Stanhope is an ideal partner for Ellen and Mr. Rudder would be an excellent husband for Abigail."

"Mother, must you?" Abigail dropped her fork onto her plate with a clatter and scowled.

Ellen tamped down a feeling of dismay. She sensed her aunt's conjectures were wrong, but the knowledge that she had been responsible for so many happy unions, most notably with her own parents, meant the reasoning for her determinations should be heard. "Please explain how you come to this conclusion, Aunt."

"Mr. Stanhope is a worthy, dependable man. His family owns an estate in Guildford, Surrey. That is only a few hours' coach ride from London. He would provide you, Ellen, with a steadfast, constant companion in life. I understand he is a second son, and he has a younger sister as well. Unlike your experience growing up as an only child, if you married him, you would have the additional companionship and support of others in his family close to your age."

"And what are Mr. Rudder's attributes that make you believe he would be ideal for Abigail?"

"He obviously shares her enthusiasm for poetry. His family home is outside Reading. Thomas and I could easily travel there. The distance would only require one night's stay at an inn. Mr. Rudder is a sensitive person, most probably a romantic. He would nurture Abigail's shy and timid nature, never neglecting her or becoming irritated by her frequent worries and apprehensions."

"I wish to point out, Aunt, neither gentleman has spoken of marriage to me," Ellen remarked, with a frown. "Has that been your experience as well, Abigail?"

"Yes. That is correct. There has been no mention of interest from either of them."

Aunt Prudence chuckled. "Some take longer than others to declare themselves. I trust, in the time there is remaining before the regatta is over, both gentlemen will realize they have found in each of you an exemplary partner for life."

Abigail came to her feet, shoving the chair away from the table with trembling hands. She faced her mother. "You must promise not to make any offhand recommendations to them!"

"Surely there can be no harm in a few incidental remarks regarding your fundamental suitability?"

"Aunt, no!" Ellen stood as well. She dropped her

serviette and reached out to grip the edge of the table. "Because of your fondness for matchmaking and your decision to turn arbitrary acquaintances into our future husbands, you have put Abigail and me in extremely awkward positions. I am sure my cousin will agree with me when I say that if this is to happen it must take place without *any* coercion from you."

"I most certainly concur! It would be quite humiliating if the gentlemen felt obligated to offer for either of us!"

The door opened and Thomas strolled into the room, carrying his gloves and top hat in one hand.

"Shall we make our way over to the theater?" He studied them. "Is something wrong?"

Abigail snorted. "Mother is insisting on promoting alliances for Ellen and me between certain gentlemen who shall remain nameless."

Thomas grimaced. "I know you have good intentions, Mother. However, in this instance, I advise you to allow the circumstances to develop spontaneously without your interference."

Aunt Prudence pressed her lips together in a firm line, contemplating Ellen first and then Abigail. She sighed. "You both know my sentiments. They were given with the best of intentions and love for you both. I will say no more on the subject. Shall we go?"

They made their way out of the room to the entry, where the butler helped them don their wraps and pelisses. After each had secured her reticule, the door was opened by Griggs. Ellen and Abigail made their way down the front stairs, followed by Thomas and his mother.

Other than a few arbitrary comments on the mild

weather and the cloudless sky, the short walk was made in silence. Just as the quietness began to make Ellen feel uncomfortable, she noticed the four Corinthian columns decorated with ornate columns, framing the large twenty-four-paned windows at the front of the King Street theater immediately ahead.

"Good evening, ladies!" Mr. Stanhope called out.

"Greetings!" Mr. Rudder added.

As they both bowed, Ellen covertly noted each gentleman's attire. Mr. Rudder's muscular arms were enclosed within the sleeves of a black, double-breasted wool frock coat with claw-hammer tails. A silver waistcoat covered his broad chest, framed by a white shirt with chitterlings and a cravat draped elegantly around his throat. His dark gray pantaloons clung enticingly to his impressive long legs. His black leather pumps had no adornments.

Mr. Stanhope wore a frock coat in dark blue. His waistcoat was gray, his white shirt plain with a stock tied around his neck. He sported black breeches on his stocky legs, cut just below his knee, with matching stockings and leather shoes with silver buckles and pointed toes.

Mr. Stanhope addressed a comment to Ellen's aunt. Thomas and Abigail studied the playbill posted on the theater's front wall.

Ellen turned to Mr. Rudder and murmured, "Did Mr. Thorne make an appearance at race practice today? There was no chance for me to question Thomas."

He frowned and pursed his lips, not answering her query.

She reached out to clutch his arm. "He did come! Was the constable called? Please, I would like to know."

He stared into her eyes for several seconds before

sighing and muttering, "It was my intention not to say anything, but I can see you will not be put off. I noticed Mr. Thorne lurking around behind the boathouse when we first arrived this morning, doubtless checking if Mr. Pratt would make an appearance. Before I could alert the race officials, he vanished. I am concerned he is following us and observing our movements. The possibility remains that he could attempt to injure one of us. As a precaution, I asked Mr. Slade to come and hover around the side of the theater tonight when the performance is finished."

Ellen took a deep, steadying breath. "I concur with your sense of disquiet and greatly appreciate the extra precautionary steps you have taken to ensure our safety. Thank you."

"Miss Cather, may I escort you inside the theater?" Mr. Stanhope stood close by with his arm raised.

She turned to him with a forced smile, at the same time hearing Mr. Rudder offer to accompany Abigail. "Yes, of course."

"I have rented a box on the left side, just above the stage," Thomas informed them, as he held his arm out to his mother. "Follow us."

Ellen and Mr. Stanhope made their way inside behind her cousin and aunt. Regardless of the fact she had been there several times before, Ellen looked around the lobby with interest, noting the lush, decorative moldings on the ceiling painted to appear as a blue sky with clouds. "You will enjoy the play, Mr. Stanhope. The interior offers optimal viewing. The theater was built in 1766, based, with some variation, on designs by James Saunders, David Garrick's carpenter at Drury Lane in London. He provided the survey plan of the Richmond

Theater in Surrey that was completed in 1765, to the Bristol architect, Thomas Paty, who supervised the construction of this building. It has similarities to the theater in Richmond due to the proportions and the proximity between the actors on the stage and the audience that surrounds them on three sides."

Mr. Stanhope chuckled. "Are you still worrying your pretty head over the tedious, masculine subjects of architecture and construction? I had hoped for a discussion with you about the *Frankenstein* story. Have you had a chance to read it?"

Ellen pressed her lips together, to stop the angry retort that threatened to burst forth from her mouth. At the same time, she chastised herself for forgetting who was at her side. It was difficult to stifle her enthusiasm over the interesting components of the theater. "Yes. I have read several chapters and reached the part where he is traveling back home to Geneva."

"Excellent! I am quite pleased to know this." He gently squeezed her hand. "What is your opinion of the tale? Has it unnerved you?"

"It is quite well written. I am less appalled by the monster than I am by his creator. I fear his fall from grace will be catastrophic, a bitter ending for someone who was once such a brilliant scientist with a promising future before him."

"I agree. The range of emotions the scientist experiences, most aptly described by the author, are quite enthralling as well as repugnant."

"Here we are. Our box should be at the top of the stairs, a few doors down," Thomas announced as he guided his mother up the carpeted steps.

They followed behind, along the wide U-shaped

passage that led to the box seats, passing several doors before Thomas stopped.

"This is the one." He pushed the door open, stepping back to allow his mother, Abigail, and Ellen to enter first.

As she followed her cousin inside, Ellen noted the six chairs that took up most of the space in the box. Three were in a row directly behind the railing, with the other chairs positioned farther back.

"I will take the seat on the inside by the wall. Abigail, you sit in the middle," Aunt Prudence decreed.

"Delightful!" Mr. Stanhope exclaimed. "Miss Cather, let me assist you to your chair. I will take my place behind. I am gratified that, from our positions, we should easily be able to take a stroll and discuss the play during intermission without disturbing the others."

"Excellent notion!" Ellen forced the words from her mouth. She had determined to attach herself to Mr. Stanhope this evening in an attempt to imagine herself living with him as his wife. She must make a genuine endeavor to discover if her aunt's conclusion that she was the best match for him was correct.

"There are not many empty seats," Abigail commented as she gazed around the auditorium. "I imagine the play has received favorable reviews?"

"Perhaps people are in town for the regatta and thought to spend the evening at the theater?" Thomas suggested.

"Whatever the reason, it is truly gratifying to see such a substantial attendance." Aunt Prudence twisted in her seat to face their group. "Before the program begins, I wished to invite you, Mr. Rudder, and you, Mr. Stanhope, to dinner tomorrow evening. Thomas informed me that Friday evening would be taken up with discussions on last-minute strategies for Saturday's regatta."

"Mr. Pratt is correct. Friday would not be possible." Mr. Stanhope paused to nod at Thomas. "I will gladly accept your invitation to dinner tomorrow night, Mrs. Pratt."

"I will also happily attend," Mr. Rudder concurred.

"Wonderful!" Aunt Prudence gave both gentlemen a warm smile. "We will sit down at the table at five o'clock, to give you ample time to return to your lodgings and rest up for your last day of practice."

"I appreciate the consideration, Mrs. Pratt," Mr. Stanhope replied, solemnly. "I look forward to the event."

"The curtain is going up!" Abigail whispered.

Ellen turned her attention to the stage. The play quickly caught her attention. The first act began with Mary Stuart imprisoned in England. The reason for her confinement was ostensibly for the murder of her husband, but it was soon apparent she had been restrained due to her claim to the throne held by her cousin, Queen Elizabeth. As Mary languished in prison, she assumed Elizabeth hesitated over signing her death sentence and began to hope for a reprieve. With the assistance of a nephew of her prison guard, she sent numerous requests to Elizabeth to meet with her to discuss the situation. In the final act before intermission, Mary gained permission for the meeting. The curtain dropped to thunderous applause.

"Enthralling!" Aunt Prudence raved as she dabbed at the corner of her eyes with a handkerchief. "Miss Desmond is a superb actress!"

"Miss Cather, shall we take a stroll in the corridor?"

Mr. Stanhope stood and held out his arm to her.

"Yes. Thank you." Ellen came to her feet and put her hand on his sleeve. As they made their way to the door, she glanced at Mr. Rudder. He had leaned forward in his chair and was deep in discussion with her aunt and Abigail.

Ellen stepped out into the passageway. She was surprised to see it was already quite crowded.

"We are not the first to leave our seats," Mr. Stanhope observed. "Come, let us make our way to the far side of the corridor, away from the stairway. It appears most people are bent on obtaining refreshments downstairs."

"I will follow your lead." Ellen replied in a perfunctory manner, her thoughts still centered on the performance.

Mr. Stanhope led her over to a small recess to one side of the main corridor. "You are quiet, Miss Cather. I trust the harsh aspects of the play have not harmed your fragile susceptibilities?"

She stared at him with her brows raised. He certainly had her attention now. "This is the second time you have concerned yourself over my supposedly vulnerable discernment. To what do you refer?"

"The unpleasant references to the grim, comfortless surroundings inside prison, the discourteous, ruthless treatment Mary is receiving. I believe your delicate mannerisms have been greatly offended."

"What do you think my image of the treatment and conditions of someone confined to a prison might be?" She only just resisted the urge to spit the query at him.

"It is not something to concern yourself with, Miss Cather," he answered in a smug manner, giving her the impression he would not welcome any further discussion on the subject. "Creditable plays for young ladies of your distinction are those that are instructive, containing the most chaste of subjects."

"Here you are!" Mr. Rudder walked up to them with Abigail at his side, her hand on his arm. "Miss Pratt tells me there is a short ballet to be performed tonight after the play has finished."

"The very thing, Miss Cather!" Mr. Stanhope answered vivaciously. "A captivating, amiable dance program will rid your mind of any coarse or disagreeable impressions you might experience after having watched such an unsuitable play."

Chapter Twelve

When the ballet came to an end, John noticed Mr. Stanhope get out of his seat and bend over to speak to Miss Pratt. He quickly stood up and walked over near Miss Cather's chair. "May I escort you outside?"

"Yes, please." She came to her feet, picked up her shawl from where it had been draped over the back of her chair, and put her hand on his arm. "We will meet you in front of the theater, Aunt."

They made their way out of the box into the crowded corridor. He took a moment to study their surroundings.

"I believe if we stay close to the wall, we will make better progress. It appears many individuals are stopping to speak to acquaintances and blocking the center passageway."

"A good observation."

John's surmise was quickly proved correct. They were able to avoid the press of people and the main stairway loomed in front of them moments later. When they stepped into the entry, he paused and turned to her. "Let me help you with your shawl."

With Miss Cather's garment securely wrapped across her shoulders, they walked outside to the front of the theater. Several patrons had already congregated there, waiting for other members of a party or for the arrival of a carriage.

Miss Cather released his arm and stepped away,

clutching the loose ends of her shawl with her gloved hands. She didn't look at him, keeping her gaze trained on some distant spot across the street.

John reached inside his waistcoat pocket and brought out the comfit tin. He flipped open the lid and offered it to her. "Would you like one?"

"No. No, thank you."

He popped one into his mouth and stowed the tin back in his pocket, wondering at the cause of her preoccupation. "I was hoping you could tell me something of the history of this building before we are joined by the others. I noticed the interior is similar to the theater in Drury Lane."

She sighed and turned to face him. "I confess my keen enthusiasm for all aspects of architecture has been dimmed substantially this evening."

He raised his brows in surprise. "How is that possible?"

"I made the mistake of expanding upon the circumstances for the final determination of the construction of this theater to Mr. Stanhope earlier this evening." She paused as her cheeks flushed pink and looked at the ground. "He chastised me for concerning myself with *masculine subjects*."

He frowned and reached out to touch her shoulder. "I am sorry he has not come around and seen fit to celebrate your interest in architecture as I have. There is no shame in having an abundance of knowledge on subjects that are considered intellectual, whether you are male or female. I greatly admire your extensive comprehension regarding the building of structures."

She lifted her head to gaze at him and give him a wobbly smile. "Thank you for saying that. It is a great comfort to me. Have you had a chance to study the book I gave you?"

"Yes, I have." He sighed. "I confess I find most of the floorplans described there have numerous advantages to them. I am more bewildered than ever!"

"If we could find an opportunity to go over the choices together, perhaps I could advise you?"

He grinned at her. "I would appreciate your help. I thought to bring the book with me tomorrow when Mr. Stanhope and I come to dinner."

She frowned. "I will endeavor to create optimal circumstances that would allow us to briefly study the options without my aunt discovering the ruse. Do not forget to wrap the book in paper."

"I won't."

The others joined them at that moment.

"A delightful evening!" Mr. Stanhope clicked his heels together and bowed. "Mrs. Pratt, Miss Pratt, Miss Cather. I look forward to the dinner. Mr. Pratt, we will see you tomorrow morning."

John bowed. "I greatly enjoyed the performances as well."

"Help!"

At Miss Cather's cry of distress, John spun around, only to see her stumbling backward against a tall, gaunt man. It was Mr. Thorne! His hand gripped her arm before he pulled it back and wrenched it behind her. The unexpected maneuver caused her to whirl in the opposite direction. She was inches away from Mr. Thorne's face, his mouth compressed and twisted with rage. "You will listen to what I have to say!"

"Take your hands off me!"

"No! Ellen! Thomas, save her!" Mrs. Pratt swooned

and fell backward against John and Mr. Pratt, effectively blocking them from reaching Miss Cather.

"Not until you convince your cousin to give up his place on the boat to me! Something quite simple for you to accomplish. I am well aware you are an outspoken wench!" The veins throbbed under the translucent skin on Mr. Thorne's face, and flimsy strands of brown hair hung damply against his sweating forehead as he spat his bitter words at her.

"Oh!" Miss Cather turned away from Mr. Thorne, hastily covering her mouth with her hand, as John imagined the smell of his foul, rotten breath threatened to overcome her.

John shifted Mrs. Pratt's bulk toward her son. "Mr. Pratt! See to your mother!"

A huge, black figure suddenly emerged from the alley. With a grunt, Mr. Thorne's hand suddenly fell away from Miss Cather's arm as Mr. Slade's giant fingers enveloped the man's throat. She staggered forward, her gloved hands stretched out in front of her.

John lunged to catch Miss Cather before she fell. He gently wrapped his arms around her, holding her against his chest. "I've got you. You are safe."

Mr. Pratt strode up to them. "Abigail is with Mother. I will see Ellen home and have a surgeon look at her arm."

"Allow me to resolve this. I promise you, Miss Cather, Mr. Thorne will never bother you again," John whispered into her ear, waiting until he felt her take a deep, shaky breath and relax against him before he lowered his arms and released her to her cousin.

"How dare you accost a lady! Where is the constable?" Mr. Stanhope fumed as he spat the words at

Mr. Thorne.

"You do not understand! My father will disown me if I do not participate in the race on Saturday! Ahh!" He gagged as Mr. Slade tightened his grip on his collar.

"Allow me to offer a suggestion." With great effort, John held his arms still at his sides to avoid pouncing on Mr. Thorne and planting his fist onto his nose. The man's actions were despicable; he had attempted to use a defenseless woman as a pawn to get his way. John took a deep breath, tamping down the intense stirrings of infuriation and anger, concentrating on the matter at hand as he quickly glanced around the area to see if they were attracting an audience. Thankfully, it appeared the groups of people nearby seemed intent on locating their carriages. "Let us make our way down the road."

"I knows where to find the constable, sir," Mr. Slade muttered, as they walked a short distance and then stopped in a secluded area behind a rise, just off the street. His large hand was wrapped around Mr. Thorne's scrawny arm. "This bloke deserves to rot in prison."

"I agree with you, Mr. Slade." John studied the gaunt, bedraggled man before him. It was hard to imagine, but before he became consumed by the need to drink spirits, he had probably been a healthy young man with a secure future before him. "Mr. Thorne has informed us he needs to be on a boat to please his father."

"Here now! That's not what I said!"

"Keep yer trap shut!" The moonlight cast an eerie light on Mr. Slade's massive fingers as he tightened his hold. "Go on, sir."

"Are you aware of any ships anchored here in Bristol that are scheduled to embark on a long voyage within the next two days, Mr. Slade?"

His bushy brows rose on his wrinkled forehead. "I does. The *Coromandel* sails with the high tide tomorrow, at eight o'clock in the morning, for Madras, India."

"Excellent! An East India Company vessel, I presume. Precisely what I was hoping for." John turned to Mr. Stanhope. "The three of us will escort Mr. Thorne to his lodgings where he will pack his bags and pen a letter to his father. He will inform him of his change of plans. Then we will head to the docks and secure his place on the ship."

"I refuse to do it!" Mr. Thorne whined.

John scowled at him. "Would you prefer to be transported to Australia and sentenced to years of hard labor? There will certainly be a vessel with that destination departing Bristol shortly."

"No, no!"

Mr. Stanhope stepped forward. "You are correct, Mr. Rudder. It is the only possible remedy to end this ongoing, grievous situation. Come, scoundrel! You are in no position to argue."

Mr. Pratt strode up to them. "What has been decided?"

"Go on ahead. I will catch up with you," John told the others before turning back to Mr. Pratt. "How is Miss Cather?"

"She is resting. I tracked down the surgeon. Fortuitously, he was making a call at the house next door. Her wrist is swollen. He fashioned a compress for her with chunks of ice wrapped in a bed sheet." He frowned. "We all want this ugly situation resolved with Mr. Thorne. Ellen asked that I return to check on what determination has been made regarding his future."

"Assure Miss Cather that she will no longer need to

concern herself with his reprehensible behavior. He sails at eight o'clock in the morning on the *Coromandel* for India."

The worried expression on Mr. Pratt's face quickly altered. The wrinkles on his forehead disappeared and he grinned. "An excellent solution! Was it your notion?"

John nodded. "I admit my knowledge of the frequent voyages on East India ships, through my uncle's connection, was the principle inducement. Once Mr. Slade verified a vessel bound for Madras was leaving tomorrow morning, all points of contention were solved."

"I imagine Mr. Thorne protested in his usual vehement manner?"

John chuckled. "He attempted to argue over his fate. You are forgetting Mr. Slade's iron-clad grip. Mr. Thorne found it hard to open his mouth without immediately knowing some form of pain and suffering."

"It appears Mr. Slade has earned the guinea after all," Mr. Pratt observed.

"I had thought of that. Mr. Slade is a determined, ornery sailor. I have a sense he will refuse payment on the grounds that he was simply assisting us to rid the city of a *drunken bloke*. I will ask Mr. Stanhope to praise Mr. Slade in his most eloquent manner for his services to us."

Mr. Pratt laughed. "He will probably accept the payment just to stop Mr. Stanhope from talking."

John grinned. "Most certainly."

"I must tell the others. Ellen will be quite relieved to hear this." He turned away with a lift of his hand. "I will see you at the boathouse in the morning."

Chapter Thirteen

Ellen woke at first light the next day and wrapped her fingers around her injured wrist. It was still tender. She sat up against the pillows and lifted her arm to better study it in the daylight and winced. There was a small, violet-colored bruise on the underside. She pushed back the blankets, sat up, and swung her legs over the side of the bed. Ignoring a slight twinge in her wrist, she reached for her wrap draped over the foot of the bed, and tossed it over her shoulders. She stood up, and on unsteady legs, made her way over to the dressing table where she splashed her face with the leftover cold water in the basin. A kernel of an idea had formed in her head last evening while Thomas related the plans that had been made to remove Mr. Thorne from Bristol. After an unsettled night deliberating all considerations, Ellen acknowledged she must be there on the dock to watch the ship sail. Knowing Mr. Thorne was traveling far away where he could never bother her again was certainly consoling. Seeing him board the ship and leave would bring her the ultimate reassurance.

She and Thomas were both early risers and usually ate together each morning. Aunt Prudence and Abigail preferred to have their breakfasts sent up on trays to their rooms. She would present herself in the dining room and request Thomas's escort. Ellen was certain he would understand the need to verify for herself that Mr. Thorne was no longer a threat to her. It should be a small matter to convince him to accompany her to the docks. As she carefully pulled one of her warmer walking gowns with long sleeves over her head, and fastened the ties at the sides, Ellen recognized there was a good chance her cousin already planned to watch the ship depart.

She quickly brushed out her tangled locks, pinning and securing them in a tight bun on the crown of her head. She pulled on her stockings and shoved her feet into her boots. Grabbing her reticule, straw bonnet, and a clean shawl from the wardrobe, she left the bedchamber, tiptoeing down the wooden stairs to the entry. With a nod to Griggs, who was hovering at his customary position near the front door, Ellen made her way down the corridor to the breakfast room. She walked inside, letting out a sigh of relief as she observed Thomas sitting at the table in front of a plate covered with several strips of bacon, a couple of eggs, and a piece of bread.

His fork made a loud clattering noise as he dropped it onto his plate. "Ellen! I had no notion I would see you this morning! How are you feeling? Is your wrist sore?"

"I am much improved. My wrist is tender and there is some bruising." She dropped her things onto a chair near the door, poured herself some tea, spooned some eggs, and dropped a piece of bread onto a plate before she took a place at the table across from him.

He frowned at her. "Should you be out of your bed? Surely, it is advisable that you rest today?"

She took a sip of tea before replying, ignoring his queries. "Thomas, are you planning to visit the docks this morning to watch the ship carrying Mr. Thorne leave port? It is imperative that I come with you."

"Yes, it was my intention…" He stopped, raising his

brows high on his forehead as he glared at her. "No! Ellen! You were cruelly attacked last night by Mr. Thorne! I dare not risk such a thing! How could I ever face your parents if you were injured again?"

"Thomas, stop! You are overstating the danger. He cannot harm me. Mr. Thorne is well guarded by not only the powerful giant Mr. Slade but also by Mr. Stanhope and Mr. Rudder, both of whom I trust implicitly."

"I cannot take you to the docks. It is unsafe. You would be vulnerable."

She studied him without speaking for a moment. "Are the wives of the departing sailors not allowed to come observe their husbands when they sail away on long voyages?"

"Of course, the wives often come to the dock to say their goodbyes."

"So, your concern stems not from the scarcity of women at that location but from a silly belief that I would be accosted by the ruffians who dally about the area. You will be my escort. Nothing will happen. Why am I not permitted to view the transport to the ship of a man who has been a source of torment to me for several days? Knowing he has truly left will soothe and relieve any possible future apprehensions I might have."

He sighed. "If doing this will provide comfort, you may come with me to the docks and watch Mr. Thorne embark for India."

"Thank you, Thomas."

They ate the rest of the meal in silence. Ellen found it difficult to swallow more than a few bites of egg and toast. Her chest felt heavy, making it hard to breathe, and her stomach clenched and gurgled with trepidation.

"I am ready." Incapable of swallowing another

morsel of food, Ellen dropped her serviette on the table and came to her feet.

"Allow me to retrieve my hat and gloves from my room." Thomas took a sip of coffee and stood up. "I will meet you in the entry."

A few minutes later, they descended the front steps of the townhouse. Thomas placed Ellen's hand on his arm.

"We will go this direction." They made their way across Queen's Square toward the center of town. "We take Anchor Road to Hotwell Road, then down Merchant's Place to the Merchant's Dock, where I understand the ship is anchored."

To calm her sense of anxiety, Ellen studied the exterior Gothic-style elevated stained-glass windows and the pinnacled decorations on the tops of the two towers as they walked past the Bristol Cathedral. One day, she intended to visit the Chapter House again. It was also located on the Cathedral grounds. It dated from 1160, and was fashioned in the Romanesque manner, its stone walls decorated with a series of intricate, patterned carvings. On her first trip there with her cousins a couple of years ago, there had been only enough time for a cursory glance at the stone carvings.

They continued past the College Green and down a side street to Hotwell Road. This was the main thoroughfare leading to the Cumberland Basin and the locks opening out to the Bristol Channel, the Avon Gorge, and then the open sea. The road was bustling with empty carts returning to the city after unloading supplies onto the ship. Just as Ellen was about to comment on the mass of vehicles, two horses jostled together for the lead spot on the roadway. One of the animals proved to be of a mettlesome disposition. The horse raised its hind legs, kicking a young groom in the head who had unwisely stepped between the two animals in an attempt to straighten out the disruption. He fell onto the dirt and didn't move.

"Oh!" Ellen gripped Thomas's arm. "The boy is hurt!"

Thomas gave the commotion on the side of the road a brief glance as he placed his hand over her trembling fingers. "There are others attending to him. You wanted to see the *Coromandel* embark. The tide is coming up. We must hurry."

Braving a last fleeting look at the youth, Ellen was gratified to see him sitting up and talking to several men standing nearby. An older gentleman bent over and offered the boy a mug of ale. Relieved to see he was getting aid, she turned back to concentrate on squeezing through the multitude of people with Thomas at her side. After much jostling, they gradually worked their way down Merchant's Place to the dock.

"There she is," Thomas declared, pointing at the ship.

Ellen stood at the railing and pushed the crown of her bonnet back off her forehead. She stared at the large vessel moored directly in front her. The deck was bustling with men of every size and shape, all outfitted in traditional sailors' garments. One man at the center of the group suddenly barked out an order and several sailors wrapped their arms around the ship's masts and shimmied up the rigging.

"Miss Cather! Mr. Pratt!"

Ellen turned at the sound of Mr. Stanhope's harried voice.

"Miss Cather, what can you be thinking by coming here? I am shocked! You, a gently reared lady, to be surrounded by a conglomeration of unsavory characters! To say nothing of the mistreatment you suffered last night."

"May I point out, Mr. Stanhope, I am accompanied by my cousin," she replied with forced composure. "My injury will heal. It was a matter of some urgency that I come here to confirm Mr. Thorne sails away on the ship."

"My cousin felt if she were here to verify his departure, it would bring her immeasurable appeasement and solace," Thomas explained.

Mr. Stanhope frowned and then pointed toward the ship. "If you need reassurance, look there. You will see Mr. Thorne standing with Mr. Rudder and the ship's captain, near the stern. We spoke to the first mate last night about his passage. The captain had not yet arrived."

Ellen shaded her eyes with one gloved hand. She saw the group of men at the rear of the vessel. The captain gestured to Mr. Thorne while Mr. Rudder reached for something in his coat pocket. "Mr. Slade did not accompany them? Is there a difficulty?"

"I don't believe so," Mr. Stanhope answered in a hearty, encouraging manner. "Merely a matter of satisfying the formalities. It is my understanding that ships of this size perpetually require additional men on board. Mr. Slade has already accepted a position."

"I imagine they must come to some type of agreement as to the capacity Mr. Thorne will occupy on the voyage," Thomas pointed out.

Minutes later, it appeared his presumption was correct. Ellen saw the captain bow to Mr. Rudder before he turned to another man standing nearby. The captain spoke to him while he gestured to Mr. Thorne. With his head bowed, Mr. Thorne followed the man and disappeared below deck.

Once he was no longer visible, Ellen looked away and gazed at the waves splashing against the side of the ship's hull. She took a deep breath as a gust of wind fanned her face. Tears began to fall from the corner of her eyes and roll down across her cheeks. She hastily wiped at them with the backs of her gloves while taking gulps of the bracing air.

"Ellen! Are you hurt?" Thomas' anxious voice sounded in her ear.

"Miss Cather? What has happened?" Mr. Rudder strode up to her and put his hand on her shoulder.

Ellen forgot her tears and stared at him with her hands suspended in front of her. A rush of delicious warmth infused her entire body. She abruptly recalled the sense of comfort and safety she had experienced when he held her in his arms the night before. A sudden, intense longing threatened to overwhelm her. She wanted to stay by his side and never, ever leave him. She loved him! "I-I am well."

"Here, take mine." Mr. Rudder reached in his waistcoat pocket and pulled out his handkerchief.

"Thank you." Ellen clutched the soft material and dabbed at her cheeks. No matter how thrilling the deep emotions she only this moment realized she had for him, it was imperative she should strive to appear calm. "Allow...allow me to explain. I resolved to come this morning to know, without a trace of doubt, that Mr. Thorne was truly gone. I had no notion his presence here in the city affected me in such an ominous, consequential manner. The solace and appeasement I experienced when I observed him disappear below deck…it took me unawares."

"I can well imagine your abundant sense of relief." Mr. Rudder smiled at her. "No doubt your cousin has told you how much the atmosphere has been lightened during practice by the absence of Mr. Thorne. Our racing prowess has improved substantially as well."

"How did you manage to get the captain to agree to take him on the ship?" Thomas asked.

"I mentioned my uncle's position in the East India Company. From there, it was simply a matter of signing a few papers."

"You will sleep well tonight, Ellen." Thomas held out his arm to her. "Let me take you home."

"I imagine you will not attend your aunt's dinner this evening, Miss Cather," Mr. Stanhope observed. "Doubtless you will not be sufficiently recovered from today's dramatic events until morning."

"I am not as delicate as you seem to believe, sir. I will most certainly be at the table tonight." Ellen couldn't stop herself from glancing at Mr. Rudder. "We have much to celebrate."

Chapter Fourteen

"Mr. Stanhope and Mr. Rudder!" Griggs announced them with a flourish as they stepped into the drawing room.

"Welcome! It is lovely to have you both join us for dinner!" Mrs. Pratt offered her hand to them from her place on the loveseat in the corner.

After greeting his hostess, John turned to Miss Pratt, who was sitting next to her mother. She was dressed in a gown of white lace covered with a striped rose-colored satin slip. Its short, full sleeves and a row of blonde lace framing the top of the bodice enhanced her natural, delicate coloring. Her thick, black hair was gathered at the crown of her head, with a profusion of loose ringlets hovering enticingly over each ear. A single strand of pearls hung around her neck.

He bowed to her. "Good evening, Miss Pratt. You look delightful."

"Thank you, Mr. Rudder."

John swiveled to face Miss Cather, who was sitting in a chair near the fireplace. Her soft, creamy skin was complimented by a light pink satin gown with short, puffed sleeves. The bottom of her skirt was finished with a band of white lace interspersed with pearls and small pink roses. Her thick blonde hair was parted in the center, the ends gathered tightly into a large comb at the back of her neck. Pearl earrings dangled from her tiny earlobes, drawing his gaze to the elegant, slender column of her throat.

He bent over her gloved hand. "Enchanting, Miss Cather!"

She stared at him and blushed, suddenly looking away. "You are too kind, Mr. Rudder."

Her agitated response and purposeful disregard troubled him. Concerned that she might believe he was trifling with her, John considered murmuring a vow of sincerity into her ear. But he was interrupted.

"Miss Cather!" Mr. Stanhope exclaimed, as he stepped forward in front of John. "Charming! I trust the injury to your wrist no longer causes you grief?"

"Thank you for inquiring, sir. I am much improved."

"I threatened to have dinner served to Ellen in her room if she put one foot outside the door after I escorted her back home this morning," Mr. Pratt commented with a grin from where he stood in front of the window on the other side of the room.

A knock sounded on the door and Griggs stepped inside, signaling Mrs. Pratt.

She came to her feet. "Dinner is about to be served. We needn't stand on ceremony this evening. Thomas, please be my escort to the dining room. Mr. Rudder and Abigail, and then Mr. Stanhope and Ellen will follow."

"Miss Pratt?" John forced a smile. He felt disgruntled after having anticipated sitting next to Miss Cather. Hopefully there would be a chance to speak privately later. Smothering his disappointment, he walked across the room and offered his arm to her cousin. They made their way out of the drawing room and into the passageway. Griggs waited for them in front of an open door at the end of the corridor.

Trailing behind his hostess and her son, John followed with Miss Pratt clutching his arm, and entered the dining room. It proved to be a large chamber with an intricate ornamental plaster ceiling edged in tiny lotus flowers and lily pads. The walls were paneled with a dark wood. An oblong table with six chairs dominated the center of the room. A large sideboard, on which a soup tureen and several wine glasses rested, occupied much of the floor space on the other side of the table. A delicate chandelier, holding at least fifteen candles, glowed brightly above the table.

"Mr. Rudder, you will sit here on my right. Abigail will be next to you. Mr. Stanhope, here on my left, with Ellen in the chair by you. Thomas will occupy the seat at the end of the table."

They took their seats, and Griggs served the soup into bowls, and then he poured wine into the glasses. After everyone was attended to, he left the room, taking the empty soup tureen with him. Two footmen entered immediately following his departure. They each carried two trays, upon which were several dishes.

"I hope you are enjoying the leek soup." Mrs. Pratt put down her spoon and took a sip of wine. "For the first course, we have salmon baked in pastry, chicken fricassee, boiled beef tongue with port wine sauce, asparagus with butter, and a potato pudding."

With assistance from the footmen, they each took a portion of food from the various dishes. The remaining bits and pieces were left on plates in the center of the table before the servants left. Griggs came into the room to ascertain all was well and to refill wine glasses.

"I imagine you enjoy a great variety of fish, living here in Bristol," John commented as he speared a piece of salmon onto his fork.

"Yes, we do." Mrs. Pratt smiled at him. "I can procure something that was caught the same morning, at a moment's notice. We certainly take the availability for granted."

"The chicken is delicious." Mr. Stanhope patted his mouth with his serviette. "Do I detect a touch of nutmeg in the sauce?"

Mrs. Pratt raised her brows. "You are correct, sir. It is a secret ingredient my cook determined to enhance the flavor of the dish. Do you spend much time in the kitchen at home, Mr. Stanhope?"

"Rarely, ma'am." He chuckled. "I believe I have an extremely sensitive palate combined with a great appreciation for food."

John turned to his other side. "Do you have a favorite dish, Miss Pratt?"

She lowered her fork before replying, "I enjoy raspberries and fresh cream. Unfortunately, it is something available only in late spring and summer."

"I had forgotten! A missed opportunity!" Mrs. Pratt exclaimed. "What a shame you gentlemen will be leaving town soon. There is a lovely vale just west of here where one may pick raspberries while taking pleasure in the delightful surroundings."

"It sounds quite pleasant. An excursion Miss Pratt must look forward to each year," Mr. Stanhope observed with a warm smile at her.

"Miss Cather, is there a type of food you have a preference for?" John asked.

She stared straight ahead of her, toward the opposite wall before looking at him. "I am always delighted to see lemon tarts served with my tea. I adore the bright, fresh taste of lemon."

"Indeed. My preference as well. Do you recall the tarts served at the wedding?" John grinned at her. "If you are ever fortunate enough to visit a home with a conservatory and orange trees, you must try almond cake with orange sugar icing if it is available. It is divine."

She pressed her lips together and closed her eyes for a moment. "Oh! The cake sounds delightful."

"Does your family home near Reading have a conservatory, Mr. Rudder?" his hostess inquired. "I recall you said your brother lives there."

"We do have a conservatory, and yes, my brother and his family reside on the estate. His wife cultivates orchids. She spends more time with her plants in the conservatory than inside the house."

"Orchids!" Miss Pratt exclaimed. "I have only seen pictures in books. I wonder if they would lend themselves to being pressed."

"Did you say pressed, Miss Pratt?" Mr. Stanhope held a spoonful of potato pudding suspended in the air.

"Yes, I did." She blushed and took a sip of her wine. "It is a ridiculous pastime of mine. I was never able to draw a flower properly. One day I decided I would collect a few specimens and press them. I started with a pansy. I believed I could better study the shape and color if the flower was fixed in one place. However, I became so enamored with the process and their beauty, even after pressing, I no longer concern myself with sketching but solely gather and press the flowers. I now have a substantial collection."

Mr. Stanhope lowered the spoon to his plate. "Miss Pratt, you will be astounded to hear my sister Leah also presses flowers in her leisure. She has derived many hours of pleasure from the occupation."

Miss Pratt's eyes widened, and she stared across the table at him. "How wonderful! Would you be interested in seeing some of my collection after dinner, Mr. Stanhope?"

"It would be my pleasure to see it, Miss Pratt."

Mr. Pratt chuckled from his spot at the foot of the table. "I warn you, sir, the assortment could take several hours to view."

John frowned. "You never mentioned your pastime when we were discussing bluebells, and you didn't gather any the day we were at Arnos Vale."

"I have always been hesitant to speak of it. As for the bluebells, the structure of a bluebell is such that pressing only tears and ruins their form," she explained. "Recall, I did request a drawing from you of a bluebell. It will be a special supplement to my collection."

"I am certain Mr. Rudder will find your specimens interesting as well. Perhaps one day we may have an occasion to visit Reading and will have an opportunity to view the orchids," Mrs. Pratt remarked, with raised brows. "Ah, here is Griggs to oversee taking away the dishes from the first remove. The second course will follow immediately. It consists of braised beefsteaks, anchovies, cabbage and spinach cake, baked apples, and syllabub."

The footmen entered the room, performing the same duties as with the first course. Once everyone had made their choices, again the excess food was left on the table in the serving dishes.

"The beefsteaks are delectable. I heartily recommend them," Mrs. Pratt advised. "Are you gentlemen staying in town next week?"

"I made plans to leave on Monday." Mr. Stanhope reached for the plate of baked apples.

John took a sip of wine. "I leave then as well."

Mrs. Pratt frowned. "It will be very quiet here next week at this time. Ellen's parents arrive Tuesday morning. She will be returning home to Richmond with them on Thursday."

Miss Cather smiled at her. "I have enjoyed my stay, Aunt."

"We always take pleasure having you." Mrs. Pratt gave a considered survey of each the occupants at her table. "If a regatta is held here next year, I hope to have the satisfaction of welcoming both of you gentlemen to Bristol again."

Mr. Stanhope cleared his throat. "I advise you to wait and see the conclusion of the race on Saturday before extending an invitation to meet once more, ma'am."

She raised her brows, her fork hovering over her plate. "Are you suggesting the outcome would be less than a flawless performance?"

He chuckled. "Oh, yes! I can pledge some imperfections."

"Mother, we will certainly do our best on Saturday, but I must remind you, our crew has only been racing together for a matter of days," Mr. Pratt pointed out.

"And that makes a significant difference to the outcome?"

"Of a certainty. Exemplary racing comes not only from strength and tenacity but also from a deep sense of collaboration and unity. That circumstance exists after working together as a crew over a period of several months," John explained.

"Thank you for enlightening me. Nonetheless, I am certain you will make a good showing on Saturday." She glanced up as the butler entered the room. "I see Griggs is here to begin clearing away. Come, Abigail and Ellen. We will leave the gentlemen to their port. You may join us in the drawing room for tea when you are finished."

"Mother, I doubt we need to be left on our own." Mr. Pratt glanced at Mr. Stanhope and then at John. "We will come with you."

John stood up and positioned himself at the back of Miss Pratt's chair, pulling it out for her. Mr. Stanhope assisted Miss Cather. Mr. Pratt escorted his mother from the room while the others trailed behind.

As they entered the drawing room, Miss Pratt released his arm, swiveling to face her brother. "Thomas, will you help me retrieve my journals of pressed flowers?"

He frowned. "Must we do that now?"

She turned to Mr. Stanhope. "Do you wish to view my collection this evening?"

"Of a certainty!" He guided Miss Cather to a chair she indicated on the far side of the room before rejoining the others. "May I help gather the journals?"

"No, no! Thomas will get them. He has done it many times before." Miss Pratt smiled. "You see, I keep them out of the way on a top shelf in the sitting room."

Mr. Pratt sighed. "Very well. I will go procure them for you."

"Thank you, Thomas. While you are gone, I will show Mr. Stanhope a few pages of the book I started some days ago." She walked over to a side table and gasped. "It is gone! Mother, where is the journal I am currently working on?"

Mrs. Pratt's eyes widened and then she let out a hearty sigh. "Oh! I apologize, my dear. I put it away in the cabinet here. I had the chambermaids dust the room earlier today and didn't want it knocked onto the floor. Here it is. Aren't the flowers arresting in their suspended conditions, Mr. Stanhope?"

John strode across the room and whispered in Miss Cather's ear. A strand of her silky blonde hair brushed against his chin. He closed his eyes for a moment, relishing the alluring scents of lavender and orange. "I trust I didn't say something when I first arrived that made you uncomfortable. You appeared upset. I assure you, my compliment was not insincere. You are a beautiful woman."

She pulled away, staring up at him briefly with eyes completely exposed and open before looking down at her hands. "I do not know what to reply, Mr. Rudder. A simple expression of gratitude in answer to such a wonderful compliment could never adequately show my appreciation. I apologize for my demeanor earlier this evening. I believe I was momentarily distracted. You were not at fault."

"I am quite pleased to know that." He studied her bowed head and the jeweled comb that held the glorious strands of her blonde hair in place. Had he imagined the longing and intense emotion that momentarily reflected in her eyes? He took a deep breath. "I have the book on the floorplans wrapped up inside my coat pocket. May we take advantage of their distraction and have our discussion?"

She straightened up in the chair and glanced at the others preoccupied with studying the journal. "Very well. We dare not open the book here. Let me have it, and I will hide it in the cupboard under some loose parchment."

He carefully pulled the volume from inside his coat. She gripped the cover with trembling fingers, got up from her chair, and went to a cabinet on the other side of the table. Quickly wedging the wrapped book underneath a pile of vellum, she closed the cabinet door and took a seat once more.

"This one is especially fine!" Mr. Stanhope enthused, from the other side of the room.

"Yes. The iris flower lends itself beautifully to pressing," Miss Pratt agreed.

"The lilacs are small, but they are quite intricate. Observe the detail!" Mrs. Pratt remarked.

Mr. Pratt entered the room carrying a stack of journals. "Here you are, Abigail. The book on the top of the pile is my personal favorite. It contains some wonderful examples of pressed hyacinths."

Miss Cather turned to John with a smile. "The others are sufficiently diverted. Are you unsure or confused about anything? We can change the subject if my aunt should come over to check on us."

He grinned at her. "I have come to a decision regarding the upper floors, the arrangement of the rooms in the basement, including the servants' hall, butler's pantry, housekeeper's room, and kitchen. I am indecisive over the organization of the ground floor rooms. Do you have any suggestions?"

"I would advise you to place the dining and breakfast rooms as close as possible to the stairs that lead down to the kitchen. I have seen several designs where this important detail was forgotten. I imagine dishes of food frequently arrived at the table cold after being carried down long passageways or corridors in those houses."

He raised his brows. "Quite an important point and something I hadn't thought of. Anything else that comes to mind?"

"Door placement is also something that can be overlooked. Do you intend to have a library and a drawing room? If so, do you prefer to have one entrance leading to the library and from there into the drawing room? Or would you wish for two separate entrances? I assume you will have a study. It is important you include a sitting room for your future wife as well. Would these two rooms have a connecting door or two separate doors opening off the main corridor? Regarding the basement; do not forget a wine cellar, a washroom, and a larder near the kitchen, besides the cook's room and butler's quarters."

He put a hand to his head. "What a countless number of details to consider and remember! It is obvious I need to purchase a book on floorplans for myself as quickly as possible."

"These flower pressings are exquisite! I wish my sister could see them," Mr. Stanhope exclaimed.

"I would advise you to make a list of the rooms you require first, separate them into the various floors, and then determine what more you require or what you have forgotten," Miss Cather suggested, with a warm smile. "I believe that process would be less confusing."

He stared into her blue eyes, noting the wide, dark irises at the center, and then lowered his gaze to her full, pink lips. Before he could stop himself, the query burst out of his mouth, "Am I to wish you and Mr. Stanhope happy?"

She frowned, looking down at her clasped hands. "No."

He studied her lowered head for a moment before murmuring, "I cannot have confused his decided attentions since the day we first encountered you in Bristol. Mrs. Pratt's sanction of his considerations was conspicuous as well."

"My aunt!" She huffed softly, and faced him, pursing her lips together. "You must be aware by now that she fancies herself a matchmaker. In fact, she was primarily responsible for my parents' marriage. Upon observing what she believed to be Mr. Stanhope's gracious deference to me, as well as your excessive courtesy to my cousin, she quickly determined to orchestrate alliances between each of us to form unexceptional, worthy duos."

"My *excessive courtesy*?" He frowned. "To what are you referring?"

"You don't recall, that first day, offering to escort Abigail to the circulating library unaccompanied by a maid?"

He stared at her with raised brows and muttered, "It's all a hum! We had just been introduced. I thought of nothing more than to offer my assistance to your cousin."

"Then you acted without giving due consideration to my aunt's motives," she whispered in an agitated, uneven tone.

He cleared his throat before answering, "An unfair aspersion! You must acquit me of any wrongdoing. At that time, I had no knowledge of her inclinations."

She shrugged her shoulders, looking away from him. "It matters not. None of us are inclined to marry, regardless of what my aunt's assumptions are."

"You believe we are all disinterested?" He pondered the side of her face, noting her flushed complexion as well as the enticing wisps of hair gathered in tiny curls against the back of her neck. "Is it possible your opinion could be changed?"

She turned back to face him, her pale blue eyes suddenly luminous. "What are you saying?"

"I have greatly enjoyed our discussions concerning construction and architecture, most especially about the optimal design of my future home." He paused to grin as her eyes widened. "It has not escaped my notice that you are equally as inspired about developing the property as I am. I would welcome the opportunity to have your assistance in the endeavor. I wish to offer you the position of my wife."

Her eyes suddenly dimmed as if they were obscured by a heavy fog. She held herself rigidly and whispered, "Do you feel you are obliged to offer for me so that I may be accepted as one of the construction crew? Are you simply indulging me, doing me a kindness with your proposal?"

He cocked a brow, confused by her reply. "Certainly. I believed you would be ecstatic at the prospect."

She sighed and lowered her gaze to the carpeted floor. "I must refuse your offer, Mr. Rudder."

A heavy weight settled upon his chest. He took a deep breath, cleared his throat, and murmured, "Surely not? I do not understand."

"A few days ago, you told me you had come to realize you were continually doing favors for others, rarely doing anything for yourself. You apologized for sounding snobbish. I will only say there are certain monumental events in life when acting in one's own interests and desires is not at all condescending. Indeed, it is the singular appropriate action one should take."

Chapter Fifteen

After a sleepless night, when jumbled, disordered thoughts and concerns crisscrossed her mind as she tossed and turned in her bed, Ellen sent a note to the kitchen asking for toast and tea to be brought to her bedchamber the next morning. Had she made the right decision when she refused Mr. Rudder's offer of marriage? She knew without question that, in this instance, her aunt's matchmaking skills had failed her. But Mr. Rudder had asked her to be his wife, believing he was offering her a good turn, an accommodation. Loving Mr. Rudder as she did, could she bear to spend the rest of her life in his company, hiding all deeper emotions, in order to provide him with a sense of satisfaction that he had brought her contentment and happiness with his proposal? It was something she could never do. She must wait and hope he decided she was equally important to his life's pleasure, not as a result of a favor but because he loved her.

A knock sounded upon the door and a chambermaid entered the room carrying a tray. Directly behind her came Abigail's maid.

Ellen directed the chambermaid to place the tray on the table near the sofa, and the girl curtsied and left the room.

"Good morning, Fanny."

"Good day, Miss Cather. Would you like me to

return after you have eaten?"

"No, no. I will not be long. I am not very hungry this morning. I requested only toast with my tea. Please remove my pink muslin morning gown from the wardrobe. I will wear the rose satin slippers."

"Very good, miss."

While Fanny procured the requested gown and additional accessories, Ellen sipped her tea and took a few bites of toast before dropping the remaining piece back onto the plate. It served no purpose to dally inside her bedchamber all morning. She would get dressed and take the *Frankenstein* book to the sitting room.

Fanny helped her don the simple gown in record time. After combing out her hair, she fastened it, with a simple twist and a few pins, to the crown of her head.

"Thank you. Please go attend your mistress. You may return later to put away my other articles of clothing."

"I have already finished dressing Miss Pratt, Miss Cather. She requested my services early this morning."

"Indeed." Ellen deliberated over this astonishing information. To her knowledge, Abigail never rose from her bed before nine o'clock. She reached for the book on her bedside table. "Carry on then."

Ellen made her way down the staircase, nodded to Griggs, and entered the sitting room. She chose a chair close to the window in order to catch the early morning light. She had opened the book and read the first paragraph of the chapter, when Abigail strolled into the room, shutting the door behind her.

"Good morning, Ellen! It is truly a lovely day!"

"Yes. Yes, it is." Surprised by Abigail's unusually cheery demeanor at this time of the morning, Ellen studied her cousin. Her eyes were radiant, the centers of the brown orbs shimmered brightly like candles. Her mouth curved upward in the shape of a crescent moon. She suddenly took a deep breath and hummed a gentle tune. Considering Abigail's normally restrained disposition, this was quite shocking. "What has happened?"

Abigail flinched and stared at Ellen as if she had forgotten where she was. "I'm sorry. I don't know what you are referring to."

"Come now! I have never seen you so chipper so early in the day. I don't recall you ever singing without being accompanied on the pianoforte. Something of note must have occurred."

She flushed and turned away, walking to stand in front of the fireplace on the other side of the room. "Perhaps I am behaving out of character. I woke up this morning with a sense of exhilaration and zeal. I could not imagine wasting another moment lying in bed."

Ellen pondered her cousin's revealing crimson countenance. Whatever the reason for the surprising change, Abigail was apparently not prepared to disclose it to her. She shrugged her shoulders and gazed down once again at the open page of the book.

"Are you reading *Frankenstein*? You must describe the story to me!"

Ellen looked up at Abigail, now standing directly in front of her with her hands clasped tightly together. "I thought you intended to read the story after I had finished it."

"Oh, yes! But I wish to begin reading it as soon as possible. I resolved to visit the circulating library at the first opportunity, to discover if they have another copy.

Please, give me a summary of what you have read up until the present point. Is it frightening?"

"No, it is not. As I explained to Mr. Stanhope, I find the story of the monster much less horrifying than the disheartening, terrible circumstances his creator must endure."

Abigail lowered her hands and gripped the skirt of her gown with trembling fingers. "You discussed it with Mr. Stanhope?"

"Yes, the evening we went to the theater. It was important that I made Mr. Stanhope aware I had procured the book after I had stated to him my intention to read it."

"Are you saying it is of the utmost significance that he acknowledges you are a person who resolves to do whatever she openly declares to accomplish?"

Ellen was confused by her question. "Of course. You know how much I value the principles of treating others with fairness and complete honesty. I would never announce an intention to do something without carrying it through to completion."

The door suddenly opened, and Aunt Prudence strode in. "Good morning, my dears! I must leave you for a few hours. Lady Walford has sent a note informing me it is imperative all the ladies on the summer fete committee meet this morning at her home, to begin discussing the food, the various performances, and sporting events. I am confident you both can amuse yourselves while I am away."

Abigail shared a smile with Ellen. "Indeed, Mother. We have plenty to keep us entertained."

"Excellent! I will see you both at tea." She turned and strode out of the room, shutting the door behind her.

The sound of Aunt Prudence's footsteps had faded away before Abigail spoke again. "Do we dare ask Fanny to accompany us to greet the gentlemen when they return to the boathouse after practice has finished?"

Ellen dropped her book into her lap and raised her brows. "The boathouse? I believed you intended to visit the circulating library."

Abigail blushed once again and stared down at her hands. "Now that Mr. Thorne is gone, I think it is important for us to support and console the remaining crew members. After all, the regatta is tomorrow."

Ellen studied her cousin, becoming more and more confused by her unusual behavior. There was also the awkward situation with Mr. Rudder. Ellen wasn't certain she was prepared to face him so soon after what had occurred last night. "You believe the gentlemen would benefit from our encouragement? I understood they intend to meet after practice today to discuss their closing strategies for the regatta."

"All the more reason to greet them immediately upon their return to the boathouse," Abigail countered.

Ellen deliberated further over her reluctance to meet Mr. Rudder. What was the cause of her sense of timidity and cowardice? Perhaps it was simply a feeling of embarrassment at the prospect of having to speak with him in a casual manner, pretending nothing of import had occurred between them. She sighed in frustration. Wasn't it Shakespeare who had a character in one of his plays lament *the course of true love never did run smooth*?

The clock on the mantel pealed ten times.

"They have just begun practice. We must change our gowns and depart as quickly as possible! Please say you will come," her cousin pleaded.

In that instant, Ellen knew she should go. One of the character traits she employed daily and admired in others was sincerity. She had treated Mr. Rudder respectably and had given him a forthright answer to his proposal. Admittedly, she had not revealed the fact that she loved him, but she couldn't live with herself if she used that information to force his hand. It made no sense to shrink from encountering him. "I will accompany you. Inform Fanny of our plans and meet me in the entry in twenty minutes."

"Wonderful!"

She and Abigail strode up the stairs together, parting at their bedchamber doors. Ellen marched into her room, shut the door, and quickly unfastened the ties on the sides of her gown. She would need to change and dress herself. Fanny would be closeted with her mistress, leaving little extra time to spend on her. Thankfully, she had requested a garment of uncomplicated arrangement to wear downstairs this morning. She quickly unfastened and stepped out of the gown, tossing it onto a nearby chair.

Going to the wardrobe on the other side of the room, Ellen pulled out the walking gown she had worn to the dock yesterday. She pulled it over her head and had secured the ties just as a knock sounded on the door and Fanny came into the room.

"Let me assist you, Miss Cather."

"Thank you. If you will brush my hair out and refasten it in the shell comb, I will wear the straw bonnet."

A few minutes later, Fanny announced she was done. Ellen stood up and thrust her feet into her half-boots. The maid secured the laces, and then handed her the hat.

"We must go." Ellen picked up her reticule and gloves from the dressing table. "Do you have my wrap?"

"I left it with Griggs in the entry."

"Very good. Let us join your mistress."

They made their way down the stairs. Abigail was waiting for them by the door. She had donned her new silk lavender pelisse, trimmed at the bottom with matching satin intertwined with twilled gauze. Her bonnet had a low crown with a large brim, hovering away from the sides of the face. Brown kid leather boots covered her feet.

"Lovely, cousin! You put me to shame. I hadn't realized we were dressing up," Ellen commented while noting Abigail's unsteady hands as she struggled to pull on her glove.

Fanny moved forward. "May I assist you, Miss Pratt?"

"No, no. Thank you." She gripped the end of the glove, thrusting her hand inside. "I have managed on my own. Shall we be off?"

Griggs draped Ellen's wrap over her shoulders before opening the door for them. Abigail put her arm through Ellen's, and they stepped out over the threshold and down the front steps with Fanny trailing behind.

"Do you recall the way to the boathouse, Ellen?"

"Yes. We walk down Prince Street to the drawbridge. We cross it. The shipyards and boathouses are down below near the basin, on the other side of the bridge."

Abigail clutched her arm as they made their way to Prince Street. "I hope the gentlemen are not angry with us for coming."

Ellen came to a sudden stop, frowning at her. "It is a little late to concern yourself with that now."

"I don't truly believe they will be cross. Perhaps a more accurate word to use would be 'surprised.' Come. We must keep moving or we will be late."

They continued down Prince Street to the drawbridge, crossing it without making any more conversation. Just as they walked down the steps and started to make their way toward the boathouse, Ellen saw a boat come around the bend in the river. It was heading to the dock.

"There they are." She had a glimpse of the back of Mr. Rudder's head as he guided the boat forward from the stroke position. Her heart rate accelerated, and Ellen struggled to breathe as she knew a moment of panic. She shouldn't have come! How was she to hide her deep emotions and feelings for him?

"Perhaps we should stand over there, by the wall, and allow them to return the equipment first?" Abigail suggested. "We can approach them later, on their way toward the bridge."

"A good notion." Ellen sighed with giddy relief as she followed her cousin. She required a few minutes to calm herself, and to recall how she had previously interacted with Mr. Rudder, a few days ago, when they were merely casual acquaintances.

They made their way around several empty boats that were perched upside down on planks in the dry dock. Fanny followed a few paces behind.

"This prospect is better," Abigail pointed out. "We can observe them without getting underfoot. When they have finished at the boathouse, we can show ourselves."

"Yes." Ellen couldn't trust herself to say anything

more. She concentrated on clenching her teeth together. She wasn't cold, but it felt as if every part of her body quivered and shook with a restrained, ardent need.

"Look! There is Mr. Stanhope. He is leaving the others! Where is he going?" Abigail put a hand on the top of her bonnet as a gust of wind blew from over the water. "I must follow him."

"Abigail!" Ellen reached out to grab her arm, but her cousin had already taken several strides away from her.

"Should I go after her, Miss Cather?" Fanny asked.

Ellen watched as Abigail approached Mr. Stanhope from behind while calling out his name. He had almost reached the steps leading to the bridge when he stopped and turned. She saw him frown and then point toward the nearby shipyards. Most probably lecturing her cousin on the unsuitability of her presence there, thought Ellen with a grimace. She turned to the maid. "No. Stay here. I imagine your mistress will be returning to this spot in a matter of minutes."

"Ellen, what are you doing here?"

She pivoted to confront Thomas. Just behind him were Mr. Rudder and Mr. Campbell. She risked a brief, yearning glance at Mr. Rudder's face. He returned her look with a bleak, melancholy expression.

"Good day, gentlemen! I hope the race practice went well. My cousin and I thought to come and greet you at the boathouse to offer our support and encouragement since the regatta is tomorrow." Ellen knew she was rambling. Where was Abigail? "How was practice today?"

"We had a strong performance, coming in second overall." Thomas stared at something over her shoulder. "Here come Abigail and Mr. Stanhope now."

"Thank you for taking the time to come and offer your reassurance, Miss Cather," Mr. Campbell spoke in his reserved, unassertive manner. He turned away as Abigail and Mr. Stanhope joined their group. "Thank you as well for your support, Miss Pratt. Gentlemen, I will meet you at the Rummer in one hour's time."

"Very good, Mr. Campbell. We will see you then," Mr. Stanhope answered. "Miss Cather, I understand this outing was not done at your instigation. I have explained to Miss Pratt that while I certainly do not concur with her notion to visit the shipyard with only you and her lady's maid as escorts, I do appreciate her gracious intention to offer reassurance and approbation to our endeavor ahead of the regatta tomorrow."

"Yes." After such a longwinded, pretentious speech, Ellen found it hard to manage a suitable reply.

"Would anyone care for a comfit?" Mr. Rudder stepped forward and held out the tin. "Miss Pratt, I don't believe you have had the opportunity to sample one yet. They are bits of clove pressed together into small pieces. Your cousin told me the aroma reminded her of a tart her nanny used to make for her."

"Thank you. I will try one." Abigail chose a small piece and put it in her mouth, savoring it for a moment before licking her lips. "Quite unique and unusually refreshing."

Thomas chuckled as he reached into the tin. "I turned down the opportunity to sample a comfit the first time you offered, but after my sister's fascinating reaction, I have to try one."

Mr. Rudder turned to her. "Miss Cather?"

"No. No, thank you." The thought of putting anything in her mouth, a moment away from breaking out into hysterics, was unthinkable.

"Mr. Stanhope?"

"What?" He appeared dazed and perplexed as he looked away from Abigail, making a conspicuous effort to train his gaze on Mr. Rudder. "Pardon? Oh, no. Thank you for offering."

"Abigail! We must go." Ellen struggled to get the words out of her mouth. She was on the brink of a nervous collapse. She had to get away. She took one step toward the bridge. Mr. Rudder blocked her way forward.

"You seem as upset and confused about your answer to my query last evening as I am. At the first opportunity, I intend to ask you again."

Ellen turned away without answering him and clutched Abigail's arm as she appeared on her other side. Oh dear! It felt as if several large boulders had just fallen across her path to true love. Would Mr. Rudder ever come to acknowledge deeper feelings for her and disentangle them?

Chapter Sixteen

"Good race, gentlemen!" John helped the others carefully drop the boat onto its wooden stand inside the boathouse. He was privately surprised they had done so well. He hadn't slept more than a couple of hours last night, and his attention was not completely on the race today.

"It's unfortunate we lost our rhythm on the final leg. We could easily have finished in second place," Mr. Pratt observed.

"We performed excellently considering the fact that, until a few days ago, we had never had an occasion to practice together," Mr. Stanhope clarified.

"Recall you hadn't picked up an oar in several years, Mr. Pratt. I believe our crew completed the course in a manner we can all be pleased with." John leaned his oars against the back wall. "Mr. Burke must be inside his office. I will inform him the equipment was returned in one piece."

"Congratulations on coming in third, John!"

He pivoted and started in surprise. "Frederick! You are here? I thought you were on your honeymoon!"

"No, no! We came back over a fortnight ago." Frederick, Lord Surd, grinned at him. "Upon our return, my wife wanted to pay a visit to her friend Miss Cather. Her mother, Lady Cather, told her she had gone to Bristol to visit her aunt and cousins. The same evening, while dining at White's, I learned you and Mr. Stanhope were also here planning to compete in a regatta. Camille and I determined we must sojourn to Bristol to cheer you on!"

"Lord Surd! I am gratified you and your wife came to watch the race." Mr. Stanhope stepped forward and bowed. "Allow me to introduce our other crew members. This is Mr. Campbell, and this is Mr. Pratt, Miss Cather's cousin."

"A pleasure, gentlemen." Lord Surd nodded to them both. "You must join me and meet the others in our party. We located Mrs. Pratt, Miss Pratt, and Miss Cather in their viewing spot on the bank near the finish line."

"The others?" John questioned with raised brows. "Are you accompanied by someone besides Lady Surd?"

Lord Surd chuckled. "As a matter of fact, several people joined our excursion to Bristol. Lord and Lady Millington and Sir Edward and Lady Collins came as well."

With a laugh, John jauntily slapped his friend on the back. "You are all here! I can't believe it!"

"I am glad I wasn't aware we had such a large group of acquaintances cheering us on," Mr. Stanhope commented, grimacing. "I certainly would have been distracted."

"We thought of that possibility, which is why I waited to inform you of our presence in town until after the regatta was over," Lord Surd replied with a smile. "Come, the others will be anxious to offer their congratulations."

"I must decline your invitation, Lord Surd." Mr. Campbell paused to clear his throat. "My intended and her parents are also in town. I must join them."

"I   perfectly   understand,   Mr.   Campbell.

Congratulations on your upcoming nuptials!" Lord Surd nodded to him.

"Thank you very much, my lord." He turned to face the others. "I enjoyed being part of your crew, gentlemen. I apologize once more for the unfortunate events earlier in the week."

"You are not to be blamed, Mr. Campbell." Mr. Stanhope came forward to shake his hand. "I am glad you were observant and took care to follow him that evening."

John nodded his head in agreement. "With your assistance, we averted a possible catastrophe."

Mr. Campbell took his leave of Mr. Pratt. With a casual wave of his hand, he walked out of the boathouse and made his way toward the Prince Street Bridge.

Lord Surd lowered his brows and frowned. "Catastrophe?"

John pursed his lips together. He would have to give his friend a brief explanation now and a more detailed account later. It was an unpleasant prospect, but it had to be done. He sighed before replying, "We were required to request our original fourth crew member, Mr. Thorne, to leave when his erratic behavior threatened to spoil our chances to compete in the regatta. We asked Mr. Pratt to join the crew. Unfortunately, our decision to drop him from the race galled Mr. Thorne so much that he determined he would pay someone to injure Mr. Pratt. Mr. Campbell noticed Mr. Thorne was acting suspiciously, eavesdropped, and informed us of his nefarious plans. Thankfully, the person Mr. Thorne believed he hired to inflict harm refused to do his dirty work."

Mr. Burke stepped out of his office at that moment.

John and Mr. Stanhope quickly completed the return of the boat and affably received Mr. Burke's words of praise for their crew's performance in the regatta.

Mr. Stanhope folded up the piece of signed parchment showing the proof of their participation and put it in his coat pocket. "I don't know about the rest of you, but I am feeling quite parched."

"I had my groom secure several bottles of ale from a nearby tavern. They are back at the viewing spot in a bucket of ice," Lord Surd declared, with a grin. "Come along."

John paired off with Lord Surd in front. Mr. Stanhope and Mr. Pratt walked behind them. He studied his friend, twirling his cane and whistling a jaunty tune as he strode along beside him. "You are in high spirits. I doubt your jubilation is due to my performance in the regatta."

Lord Surd chuckled. "Goodness, no! Although you carried out your duties in the extremely important stroke position in the most commendable manner."

"Thank you for your exceedingly gracious praise. What then is the source of your animated disposition?"

"You do recall I recently married?"

"Yes, I remember the occasion. I attended the ceremony only last month!"

"You know the inducement for my joyful temperament then."

"Your wedding? You surprise me! Of course, I imagine it is quite gratifying to be joined in matrimony to a woman you maintained a close friendship with for many years."

"Friendship?" Lord Surd raised his brows. "At the beginning of our acquaintance I suppose our relationship could be described as one of mutual amicability and rapport. I love my wife. I could not imagine experiencing the sort of happiness and deep, long-lasting emotion I feel for her today if she were simply a friend."

"Love?" John frowned and then his expression cleared. "You refer to a sense of affection, a strong regard for someone who is your life's partner. People in our class rarely marry for love."

"Indeed." Lord Surd studied him for a moment without speaking. "What of your brother? I understand he is married with a wife and children. Is he happy?"

"Charles?" He shrugged. "I wouldn't describe his demeanor in that way. I would say he is content. Their marriage was ordained immediately after his wife was born. Her family owns the property next to our estate."

"Your mother and father? Did they have an arranged marriage?"

"No. It is my understanding they met in the usual manner, at a ball in my mother's first season. I rarely see them together. They both maintain extremely active social schedules."

"Mr. Rudder! Congratulations!" Lady Surd approached them with a wide smile on her face. She turned to her husband and her lips parted. She reached out to stroke his arm with her gloved hand. "Frederick."

Lord Surd bent over his wife, appearing to inhale the scent of her hair.

"Thank you, Lady Surd." John bowed while noting his friend's poignant response to her. "It is lovely to see you again."

"My dear." Lord Surd spoke to her softly, the words were a warm caress. He stared down at his wife for a moment before clearing his throat and putting one hand at her back to turn her. "Look who else is part of the rowing team. You remember Mr. Stanhope? And Mr. Pratt. He is Miss Cather's cousin."

"Of course, I recall Mr. Stanhope from our summer at Horsham House. My compliments to you and Mr. Pratt for an excellent race today!"

"Thank you very much, Lady Surd," Mr. Pratt answered.

"A pleasure, Lady Surd!" Mr. Stanhope bowed over her hand.

"Come greet Lord and Lady Millington and Sir Edward and Lady Sophia," Lord Surd urged as he placed his wife's hand on his arm.

John followed the others over to the spectator enclosure located just above the regatta course. Many of the people who had come to view the race had already left, but there were a few groups scattered about enjoying celebratory food and drink with crew members from other boats. Lord and Lady Millington were seated on chairs underneath a large elm tree. Her gloved hand rested securely in her husband's palm. Sir Edward and Lady Sophia sat on a blanket just in front of them. Sir Edward had one arm draped across his wife's shoulders. Mrs. Pratt sat in a chair on the other side of Lady Millington. Miss Cather was next to her. Miss Pratt reclined on a blanket off to one side.

"Here they are!" Lord Surd called out as they walked up to the gathering.

"Congratulations!" A loud chorus of cheers sounded from everyone.

"Thank you all! It is wonderful to have so many friends here to celebrate our competent finish in the race today." Mr. Stanhope easily took on the role of crew spokesman.

"Come with me while I instruct my groom to distribute some bread, cheese, and the ale," Lord Surd said to John while leading his wife to a chair next to Miss Cather. Once Lady Surd assured him she was comfortable, he continued to John, "I have a sense there is more to the story concerning the outcast crew member."

John scowled. "Yes, there is. I hesitate to ruin the day and elaborate on it. Let me just say that we put him on a ship bound for Madras, India, on Thursday morning."

Lord Surd raised his brows. "A most effective method of removing an unwelcome individual causing discord as well as chaos."

"He will not return to these shores for many months, if ever," John vowed, choosing not to say more about Mr. Thorne's abhorrent, desperate attempt to harm Miss Cather.

Lord Surd gave his instructions to the groom, and they returned to their group of friends who were chatting with each other in the enclosure. John noticed Mr. Stanhope had taken a place on the blanket next to Miss Pratt. Lady Surd and Miss Cather were deep in conversation. Mr. Pratt was speaking with Lord and Lady Millington. Sir Edward raised his arm, hailing him.

John strolled over to their blanket. "It is wonderful to see you both."

"Pull up a chair, Mr. Rudder." Sir Edward turned to his wife. "Sophia and I were wondering why we hadn't come across you when we visited London last week. We were surprised when Lord Surd told us you were in Bristol."

He chuckled. "I hadn't planned to be here. Mr. Stanhope asked me to do him a favor and join the race crew a fortnight ago when the fourth member could no longer compete."

"You often come to the assistance of your friends, Mr. Rudder," Lady Sophia pointed out. "You graciously agreed to witness our wedding ceremony as well."

"That is correct." He grinned at them. "You will be gratified to know I plan to do something for myself now that I have finished providing my assistance here."

Lady Sophia sat up straight, looking directly at him with raised brows. "Do you intend to marry? You, Miss Cather, and Mr. Stanhope are the only ones left from the summer retreat a couple of years ago who remain single."

"No. I thought to…. No matter." He paused to take a calming breath. "My father has given me a substantial piece of property, once owned by my grandfather, near Rochester in Kent. The original structure, a hunting lodge, burned down years ago. I plan to build a home on the land overlooking the lake."

"Excellent!" Sir Edward reached across the blanket to tap him on his knee. "If you should need to reference builders' pattern books or would like to study Greek architecture, I have several volumes on the subjects in my library at Horsham House. They were part of my father's collection."

"I appreciate your offer. Miss Cather told me about the books."

"Did she?" Sir Edward grinned. "We were discussing the history of Horsham House one day during the summer retreat. Miss Cather was delighted when I mentioned my father's reference books. She spent every free moment she had studying them."

"You've discussed your plan to build a house with Miss Cather?" Lady Sophia asked, with a smile.

"Yes, I did. She provided me with several excellent suggestions regarding its construction and design."

"Good day, Mr. Rudder! Bring your chair over," Lord Millington suggested. "My wife and I would like to congratulate you. We secured a pint of ale for you as well."

John turned to see them both gesturing to him. Mr. Pratt had joined Frederick and his wife. He excused himself to Sir Edward and Lady Sophia and carried his chair over, setting it down close to their seats. "A pleasure, Lord and Lady Millington."

"I apologize for not coming over to join the group." Lady Millington glanced at her husband and blushed.

"My wife is *enceinte*," Lord Millington murmured as he handed John a pint. "I want her to stay off her feet as much as possible."

"Congratulations!" John smiled at them both. He took a sip of the ale.

"Thank you." Lady Millington studied him. "Did I hear you discussing building a home?"

"Yes. My father recently gifted me a large parcel of land. I plan to construct a house there."

"Lucas and I finished remodeling the nursery wing a few months ago." She gave her husband a warm smile. "It was a marvelous experience."

"I can imagine it would be convenient," John paused to clear his throat and take another drink, "and quite expedient as well, to have an interested partner working alongside to smoothly complete the process."

Lord Millington sat up straight against the back of

his chair, reaching for Lady Millington's hand. "Convenient and expedient? I would never associate those words with the time I spend with my wife. Captivating and delightful are two that come to mind."

John had a sudden image of Miss Cather, when they were discussing the various options for his future home, her blue eyes twinkling, her full red lips curved in an enchanting smile. Something loosened inside his chest. He took a gulp of air and turned to glance at the group of chairs where he had last seen Miss Cather. She was gone. He searched the surrounding area and noticed her standing on the edge of the nearby walkway, facing the water. John dropped the mug and surged to his feet. "Excuse me. I must rectify a most grievous choice of words."

****

"It has been lovely making your acquaintance, Lady Surd," Aunt Prudence gushed. "I had no idea so many of the attendees at the country house party two years ago had married, and so happily as well. I had hopes Mr. Stanhope and Ellen would come to see their suitability for one another, but I don't believe anything monumental has occurred between them that would be an indication of a promising, lasting relationship."

"Excuse me." Ellen stood up and walked toward the water. She couldn't sit still listening to her aunt's arbitrary matchmaking schemes any longer. She stopped at the edge of the quay and took a deep breath, attempting to concentrate on the boats bobbing up and down in the water in front of her.

"May I speak to you a moment, Miss Cather?"

She turned and stifled a gasp. Mr. Stanhope stood directly behind her, holding his hat in one hand, his face flushed and his stance awkward, as he shuffled both feet back and forth on the loose gravel covering the pathway.

"Yes, you may. Is something wrong?"

He gripped the brim of his hat in his hand and pursed his lips. "I do not wish to cause you pain. That was never my intention. I consider myself a constant, unwavering individual, but I recently experienced a sudden, remarkable form of comprehension that caused me to change what I believed was an unalterable, fixed design."

Ellen wrinkled her brow as she tried to decipher his implications. "Are you saying you received disconcerting news from your family?"

He grimaced. "No, not at all! When I inform them what has happened, I expect my family will be elated. I wanted you to be the first to be apprised—your cousin has agreed to my request to pay my addresses to her."

"Abigail?"

"Yes. Provided Mrs. Pratt and her brother, Mr. Pratt, give their blessing to our eventual union."

Ellen felt a sudden sense of giddiness; a great satisfying warmth spread throughout her body. She wanted to open her mouth and sing, to shout and laugh all at the same time. Instead, she smiled. "My aunt will be overcome by surprise, but she will quickly come around. She and Thomas will be thrilled with the news."

"And you?" He studied her. "I believed… You are so capable, Miss Cather, and never require advice or assistance."

"My sweet, sensitive cousin is perfect for you. You will enjoy looking after her and protecting her. Abigail will always value and appreciate your defense of her and your attention to her needs." She grinned at him. "You have come to realize I would be miserable under such incessant consideration."

"And I would have been frequently provoked and exasperated by you." He smiled and held out a gloved hand to her. "I hope we can always be friends?"

"Of course." She placed her hand in his. "We will soon be family as well."

He chuckled as he released her hand. "I hadn't thought of that. Wonderful. I am certain I will see you later."

"Until then."

Ellen sighed as he walked away, and she moved forward to the edge of the path. She studied two seagulls as they swooped down low over the water. Mr. Stanhope would be good for Abigail. Their union would certainly flourish.

"I wish to start over."

She whirled again, this time to the sound of Mr. Rudder's voice. He stood close behind her, his expression glum as he gazed at her from under half-open eyelids.

"Start over?" she inquired.

"Yes." He took a step forward, taking a deep breath, lifting his head, looking directly into her eyes. "Yesterday I told you I intended to offer for you again. In my mind, I had my proposition completely refined and polished. The advantages and benefits to your capacity as my wife would be so obviously numerous you couldn't possibly turn me down. And then today happened."

She frowned. "Today? Are you speaking of the regatta?"

"No." He clenched his fingers together into fists and

turned away from her. "I am sorry. When I recall what I said to you when I offered you the position of my wife…. You must have thought me the worst kind of oaf! An insensitive, blundering fool!"

"Never that." Ellen reached out to tug his arm, impelling him to face her. "You believed you were offering me an indulgence. I would be given a rare opportunity to immerse myself in something I have great interest in and fascination for. You do understand what I was trying to say? I meant I could never be your wife under those circumstances."

"I comprehend everything now. I was offering you an accommodation, a favor. Before today, it was my way of showing, to the people I cared for, my dependable, trustworthy nature. But something was missing. I realize that now. There was no sincere emotion involved. Today—this afternoon, to be more precise, from the moment Lord Surd and I left the boathouse, chatting together—I have been surrounded by people who savor experiencing deep emotions, couples who hold each other dear. They truly cherish one another. Once I recognized that, something suddenly came unlocked, and I felt a kind of joyous freedom deep inside of me." He reached out to take hold of her hand. "I thought of you, of our intriguing, fascinating conversations, your lovely smile, your beautiful blue eyes. I knew, with absolutely no sense of confusion or bewilderment, that I love you, Ellen."

"I love you, John. You recognize now why I couldn't marry you without knowing you felt the same way about me?"

"Yes. Yes, most certainly I do." He sighed, a long, low moan. He released her hand and wrapped his arms around her waist, leaning in to kiss her.

Ellen reached up to intertwine her arms around his neck, relishing the wonderful, extraordinary sensations coursing throughout her body as his warm lips covered hers, taking additional exquisite, sweet pleasure in his embrace, knowing that he loved her.

He lifted his head and stared down at her. "I am eager to begin our lives together. I will speak to your father soon after your parents arrive."

"How advantageous that you have already attended an expeditious marriage ceremony. It should be a simple matter to plan our own," Ellen teased as she gazed adoringly up into his shimmering hazel eyes. She reached up to push a lock of his hair off his forehead. "My aunt is going to be quite perplexed. Her matchmaking skills seem to be dwindling away. Mr. Stanhope informed me a few minutes ago that Abigail has accepted his suit."

"Your cousin and Mr. Stanhope? Well, well!" He grinned down at her. "I have a sense your aunt will quickly adjust the scope of her attentions. I see a title of wedding advisor in her future!"

A word about the author…

Cynthia Moore grew up in a small, southern California beach town. While many hours were spent lying on the sand, she always had a book in hand or a paperback tucked inside a bag ready to pull out and read after a quick splash in the waves. Cynthia discovered British literature as a teenager. After reading most of the Victorian classics, she was introduced to English Regency period novels in 1987. It was love at first read. Since that time, Cynthia has read over four thousand fiction novels and owns a large collection of research books about the fascinating era. She is extremely proud to have several published stories set during the Regency and resides in Southern California with her dog who is, not surprisingly, named Austen.

www.cynthiamooreauthor.com